THE DAUGHTER'S ENDURING LOVE

The Victorian Love Sagas
Book 5

Annie Brown

The Daughter's Enduring Love — Annie Brown

Copyright © 2024 Annie Brown

The right of Annie Brown identified as the author of this work, has been asserted in accordance with the Copyright Designs and Patents Act 1988.

All rights reserved. No part of this work may be reproduced in any material form (including photocopying or storing by any electronic means and whether or not transiently or incidentally to some other use of this publication) without write permission of the copyright holder except in accordance with the provisions of the Copyright, Designs and Patents Act 1988.

Applications for the copyright holder's permission to reproduce any part of this publication should be addressed to the publishers.

Contents

1. Chapter 1 — 1
2. Chapter 2 — 11
3. Chapter 3 — 14
4. Chapter 4 — 25
5. Chapter 5 — 28
6. Chapter 6 — 32
7. Chapter 7 — 37
8. Chapter 8 — 40
9. Chapter 9 — 44
10. Chapter 10 — 47
11. Chapter 11 — 51
12. Chapter 12 — 56
13. Chapter 13 — 59
14. Chapter 14 — 68

15.	Chapter 15	75
16.	Chapter 16	81
17.	Chapter 17	84
18.	Chapter 18	88
19.	Chapter 19	94
20.	Chapter 20	98
21.	Chapter 21	102
22.	Chapter 22	108
23.	Chapter 23	112
24.	Chapter 24	114
25.	Chapter 25	120
26.	Chapter 26	124
27.	Chapter 27	129
28.	Chapter 28	132
29.	Chapter 29	139
30.	Chapter 30	148
31.	Chapter 31	151
32.	Chapter 32	159
33.	Chapter 33	167
34.	Chapter 34	171
35.	Chapter 35	174
36.	Chapter 36	176
37.	Chapter 37	179
38.	Chapter 38	182

39.	Chapter 39	184
40.	Chapter 40	187
41.	Chapter 41	190
42.	Chapter 42	195
43.	Chapter 43	202
44.	Chapter 44	207
45.	Chapter 45	211
46.	Chapter 46	215
47.	Chapter 47	219
Epilogue		226
About the author		229

Chapter One

Hetty Morgan's fingers quivered as they brushed against the cold, still cheek of the man laid out on the preparation table before her.

The sombre dance of shadows cast by the gaslight lamps played across his features, giving him a haunting semblance of life that sent a shiver down Hetty's spine.

The scent of embalming fluid clung heavily in the air, its harsh acridity mingling with the faint but ever-present smell of coal dust that seeped in from the bustling streets of Blackstone. Even here, within the confines of the undertaker's parlour, there was no escape from the industrial grind that choked the town.

'Father says it preserves them, keeps the decay at bay,' Hetty muttered under her breath, echoing the words often spoken by her father in justification of their morbid trade. She couldn't help but wonder if anything could preserve the remnants of her own hopes and dreams, which seemed to wither a little more each day in this place of death.

"Hetty, make sure you've filled the cavities well. We can't have any incidents during the service," Mr Morgan, her father, called out from the ledger he was hunched over at the back of the parlour.

"Of course, Father," Hetty replied, her voice steady despite the fluttering in her chest. She reached for a bottle labelled with precise, faded handwriting and poured the preserving fluid with a meticulous hand. There was an art to this, she supposed, a macabre one that needed both a steady hand and a steeled heart.

"Blackstone won't tolerate mistakes, not with everything that's been happening," her father continued, the weight of their reality clear in his tone.

Hetty nodded, though he couldn't see it, her thoughts turning to the whispered rumours of resurrectionists and the unease that had settled over the town like fog on the Thames. She dipped a cloth into the fluid and began to wipe down the pale skin of the corpse, her movements gentle and reverent.

"Have you heard from the Yardleys? I hear they're looking for someone," Hetty ventured, a subtle plea laced within her words for a life beyond these walls.

"Stick to what you know, Hetty. We have our duties here," came the curt reply, closing the door on the conversation as surely as they closed the coffins on those they tended to.

'Steady now,' she whispered to herself, taking a deep breath that did little to calm her nerves. Her deft, practised movements belied the dread twisting in her gut. With each careful stitch, she secured the

shroud around the body, ensuring the deceased would be presentable for his final journey.

Hetty bowed her head, focusing on her task, the delicate balance between duty and desire weighing upon her like the coffins they crafted. Silence once again settled over the parlour, broken only by the occasional creak of wood and the whisper of fabric as she continued her grim work.

Thomas Morgan's shadow preceded him as he pushed the heavy door open, a sliver of outside light momentarily piercing the gloom of the room before surrendering to the darkness. His footsteps were soft, yet each one seemed to press down on Hetty's spirit with the heaviness of the coffins they housed.

"Hetty," he said, his voice barely rising above the stillness, "the stitches on Mrs Clarendon's shroud are crooked."

She followed his gaze to the shrouded form laid out before her. "It's nothing a few adjustments can't fix," Hetty replied, masking her frustration with a calm she did not feel.

Her father sighed, and in the dim light, she saw the furrows carved deep into his brow. His eyes, once keen and bright, now carried the burden of their secret commerce, a reflection of the toll it took on both of them.

"Is it ever enough, Father?" Hetty's fingers hesitated over the fabric. "The lengths we go to just to keep—"

"Enough to survive, Hetty," he interjected, his tone brooking no argument. "We do what we must."

There was love there, in the lines of his worn face, love that had become entangled with duty and despair. Yet resentment brewed within her, a bitter potion that threatened to poison the bond they shared.

"Survival is not living," she murmured, more to herself than to him, her voice barely audible.

"Living?" Thomas scoffed softly, the sound hollow in the cavernous room. "Luxuries are for those who can afford dreams, not for us."

Hetty looked down at her hands, her skin stained by the work, a stark contrast to the ivory lace of her childhood fantasies. Her heart ached with the realisation that every passing day drew the shutters tighter on the world she longed for. She imagined a life filled with a heartwarming love for a husband she could only wish for, books and laughter instead of the sombre silence of death.

"Father, I—" her voice broke, revealing the chasm that yawned between her yearnings and reality.

"Hetty." Her name on his lips was a plea, an acknowledgment of her unspoken sorrow. He stepped closer, and for a fleeting moment, she thought he might reach out to comfort her.

But he only straightened his back, as if bracing against the tide of emotions. "Finish your work. There will be more bodies coming before dawn."

She nodded, a single tear escaping to track down her cheek, its warmth a cruel contrast to the cold touch of mortality that surrounded her. With diligent hands, she corrected the stitches, her dreams sewn tightly within the folds of the shroud, buried along with the dead.

The sharp rap of knuckles against wood sliced through the hush like a scalpel, jolting Hetty from her thoughts. Her father's head snapped up, and they exchanged a glance, both sets of eyes wide with unspoken apprehension.

'*Who would call at this late hour?*' Thomas Morgan muttered under his breath as he moved toward the door, his footsteps soft but heavy on the threadbare carpet.

Hetty set down the needle and thread, her hands now still but for the tremor that betrayed her tension. She lingered by the table, hoping to glean snippets of the conversation about to unfold.

The door creaked open, and Mr Grayson, the local coroner, slipped inside. His voice was low, a susurrus that murmured through the chilled air, punctuated by the staccato of her father's terse responses.

"Thomas, the death toll's rising," Grayson intoned, his words barely reaching Hetty's ears.

"Is it the fever again?" The concern in her father's voice carried clearly to where she stood, veiled in shadow.

"Hard to say." Grayson's reply was edged with unease. "But I fear we're facing something darker than disease."

A shiver ran down Hetty's spine, chasing the warmth from her flesh. She pressed closer to the wall, her gaze fixed on the two men outlined by the flickering lamplight. Something sinister was brewing in Blackstone, and their family stood at the heart of it.

The thud of the official's boots reverberated through the floorboards, each heavy step a drumbeat that resonated with Miss Hetty Morgan's racing heart. She peered from behind the curtain of her auburn hair, watching as Mr Grayson's silhouette loomed larger and more ominous with his approach. The air seemed to grow colder, heavier, bearing down on her with the weight of their unsavoury livelihood.

"Mr Morgan," the official's voice was stern, "we must discuss the arrangements for these unfortunate souls."

Her father, his face drawn with lines of exhaustion and sorrow, nodded. "Of course, Mr Grayson. We always provide our services with the utmost discretion."

"Discretion, yes," Grayson agreed, though unease crept into his tone. "But the rumours, Thomas. They are spreading like wildfire through the town."

Hetty clutched at her skirt, the fabric wrinkling under her tense grip. Her eyes flitted between the two men, reading the subtext woven into their careful dance of words. The fear was palpable now, an uninvited guest that had taken up residence in her mind.

"Rumours have always been as common as rats in this town," her father replied, but the defiance in his voice did little to mask the concern that flickered in his weary gaze.

"Perhaps," conceded Grayson, "but when whispers turn to cries of outrage, we must take heed. The people demand answers, they demand..."

"Justice?" Thomas Morgan interjected, a hint of steel sharpening his usual deference.

"Peace, Thomas," Grayson sighed, the façade of officialdom slipping. "We all seek peace, but how can there be any, with this dark cloud of death hanging over us?"

Hetty felt the stirrings of dread coalesce into a tangible threat. The dead, once silent, now spoke volumes, and their voices were stirring unrest in the streets of Blackstone. She stepped forward, the impulse to intervene battling with her ingrained restraint.

"Father," she began, voice barely above a whisper, "perhaps we should—"

"Hetty, child," her father cut her off with a gentle but firm hand raised in her direction. "This is a matter for Mr Grayson and me."

She fell back, silenced, but her mind raced. The implications of their trade with the dead, the increasing toll, the whispers of fear—it was all too much, threatening to swallow the last vestiges of normalcy they clung to.

"Very well," Grayson said after a moment of contemplation. "We shall continue as we have. But be warned, the eyes of Blackstone are upon us, more now than ever."

With that, the official turned on his heel, his departure marked by the diminishing echo of his footsteps. Left in the wake of his words, Hetty watched her father slump ever so slightly.

"Father," she murmured, "what will become of us?"

Thomas Morgan met his daughter's gaze, his eyes reflecting a shared turmoil. "We will endure, Hetty. As we always have." But his reassurances rang hollow in the shadowed room, where the scent of embalming fluid lingered like a ghostly reminder of the mortality they were surrounded by.

In the silence that followed Mr Grayson's departure, Hetty turned away from her father and busied herself with the task at hand. The stillness of the room was broken only by the sound of her father meticulously recording the details of their latest client in his ledger. As she worked, Hetty's mind wandered to a time before death had become her daily companion.

"Father," she said softly, breaking the hush, "do you remember when I used to teach the younger children their letters?"

Thomas looked up, his quill pausing mid-stroke. "Of course, my dear. You've always had a way with them."

A small, wistful smile graced Hetty's lips. "I dreamt of having my own classroom one day. Rows of eager faces, chalk dust swirling in the sunlight. It seemed a noble calling."

Her father's expression softened for a moment before he closed his ledger with a sigh. "Hetty, we have our place, and we must do what is necessary."

She felt the sting of those words, even as she nodded in understanding. "I know, Father. I just can't help but wonder what life would be like beyond these walls."

"Hetty," he continued, his tone laced with disapproval, "I cannot afford distractions. Your fantasies will not put food on the table or keep this establishment running."

Hetty's cheeks flushed with embarrassment, and she lowered her gaze. "I'm sorry, it won't happen again."

"See that it doesn't," he admonished. "We need to be vigilant. These are trying times, and our livelihood depends on discretion and dedication," Thomas replied, his eyes meeting Hetty's for a brief second before returning to his work.

Hetty bit her lip, the weight of unfulfilled aspirations heavy in her chest. She took a deep breath and focused once more on the task before her, the vision of chalkboards and smiling children fading into the shadows of the undertakers.

"Remember, Hetty," her father's voice was soft but carried an undercurrent of urgency, "our work here is both necessary and misunderstood. We provide a service, albeit one that society prefers not to acknowledge or discuss."

She nodded, "I am well aware, Father. The whispers, the looks we receive when we walk through Blackstone—they are constant reminders."

"Indeed," Thomas sighed, his gaze lingering on the corpse before them. "The dead tell no tales, but the living are not so discreet. Our role in this town is a precarious one; respected for our necessity yet reviled for the nature of our trade."

As if summoned by their conversation, a burst of laughter echoed from outside, youthful and carefree. Hetty paused, her heart tightening at the sound. A group of children played in the street, their voices carrying through the slightly ajar window, untainted by life's grimmer realities.

"Listen to them," she murmured almost to herself, a wistful note in her words. "They know nothing of this world we're bound to."

"Their innocence is a luxury," her father replied, his tone revealing a hint of something—regret, perhaps? "One day they may understand, but for now, let them enjoy their childhood. It is fleeting."

"Of course." She straightened her spine, setting aside the longing that clawed at her heart. The children's laughter was like a ghost, haunting her with memories of a simpler time. But she was a Morgan, and Morgans did not succumb to idle reverie.

Hetty's hands paused over the shroud she was pinning, her mind drifting to a time when warmth and laughter had filled their home. "Mother would have chided us for working in such silence," she said softly, not looking up from her delicate work.

Her father's hands stilled as well, and he turned his weary gaze upon her. "Yes," he agreed, the rough timbre of his voice softening. "She always preferred music to quiet. Said it made even the darkest days brighter."

"Remember how she'd hum a tune while baking? Her voice would fill the entire house." Hetty allowed herself a small smile, the memory like a balm to her soul.

The moment of shared tenderness faded as quickly as it had appeared, leaving a chill in its wake. Hetty felt the familiar weight of responsibility settle back onto her shoulders.

"Father," she said at last, her voice steady despite the turmoil within, "I will always stand by you, but I cannot pretend it does not wound me—to be scorned for giving dignity to the dead."

"Hetty," he replied, his eyes meeting hers with an intensity that belied his stoic facade, "you are my greatest pride. And the day will come when the world sees your worth as clearly as I do."

Until then, they were bound by blood and burdened by a legacy that granted them neither peace nor prestige.

And with the echo of innocent mirth just beyond the walls, Hetty returned to her grim duties.

Chapter Two

The pale morning light filtered through the lace curtains of Hetty Morgan's bedroom, casting delicate shadows across her face as she stirred from her slumber. For a moment she allowed herself to linger in the peaceful realm between sleep and wakefulness, before the weight of her reality settled upon her once more.

With a soft sigh, Hetty rose and began her daily ritual. As she pinned her auburn hair into a modest bun, her eyes fell upon the small portrait of her mother on the vanity. A familiar ache bloomed in her chest, a mixture of longing and determination that had become her constant companion.

"Another day, Mother," she whispered, touching the frame gently. "Another day to make you proud."

The floorboards creaked beneath her feet as she made her way downstairs, the sound a reminder of the age and history embedded in the very bones of their home. The scent of strong coffee and freshly baked bread greeted her, a small comfort amid the lingering undertones of formaldehyde and sadness that seemed to permeate every corner of the Morgan residence.

Her father was already at the kitchen table, poring over his ledgers with a furrowed brow. He looked up as Hetty entered, offering a tired smile that didn't quite reach his eyes.

"Good morning, my dear," he said, his voice rough with fatigue. "I trust you slept well?"

Hetty nodded, pouring herself a cup of coffee before joining him at the table. "As well as can be expected. Any business today?"

Thomas's face tightened almost imperceptibly. "I heard this morning. The Widow Hawkins passed in her sleep. We're to collect her before noon."

Hetty's heart sank. Mrs Hawkins had been kind to her, always offering a warm smile and a piece of candy when Hetty passed her little shop. Now, she would be just another body, another entry in her father's books.

"I'll prepare the carriage," Hetty said, rising from her seat.

Her father's hand on her arm stopped her. "Hetty," he began, his voice hesitant. "You know, if this life is too much for you... if you wish to pursue other interests..."

For a moment, hope flared in Hetty's chest. Images of a different life – of marriage, of books and learning, of a classroom full of eager young minds – danced before her eyes. But then reality reasserted itself. She saw the lines of worry etched into her father's face, the weight of responsibility that bowed his shoulders.

"No, Father," she said softly, squeezing his hand. "My place is here, with you. This is our duty, our calling."

Thomas nodded, relief and something like regret mingling in his gaze. "You're a good girl, Hetty. Your mother would be proud."

As Hetty stepped out into the crisp morning air to prepare for the day's grim task, she couldn't shake the feeling that she was standing at a crossroads. The path before her was shrouded in shadow and uncertainty, but she squared her shoulders and pressed on. She was Hetty Morgan, the undertaker's daughter, and she would face whatever challenges lay ahead with courage and grace.

Little did she know that fate was already conspiring to test her resolve in ways she could never have imagined.

Chapter Three

"Hetty? Hetty!"

"Yes, Father?"

"I have run out of arsenic, can you visit Dr Carter and ask that he lends us some, enough for a week will do."

"When, Father? I have Mrs Blanchstone to attend to this morning."

"That will wait, this is more important."

"I'm surprised you have run out, it's not like you."

"Yes, well, I have things on my mind that I dare not speak about and are none of your concern."

"Is it to do with Mr Grayson's visit yesterday? I noticed the conversation was more agitated towards the end."

"I said, it's none of your concern. Now please, do as I ask and visit Dr Carter, he will be accommodating I am sure."

At the simple mention of his name, Hetty's heart flickered abnormally just for a moment, but long enough for her to realise that her feelings for him had not changed since the first time they had met.

Hetty nodded in agreement with her father and requested the carriage be brought around to the front of the workshop. As she waited, her fingers absently traced the worn velvet of her gloves—a remnant of finer days.

The carriage, once a symbol of the Morgan family's prosperity, now stood as a bittersweet reminder of their changed circumstances. Its polished wood and brass fittings, though slightly tarnished, still hinted at a bygone era of comfort and social standing.

"Where to, Miss Morgan?" inquired the coachman, his tone respectful despite the visible patches on his livery.

"Dr Carter's office please, thank you," Hetty replied, her diction clear and measured, a vestige of her mother's careful tutelage. "I shall be with you in a moment."

Hetty hurried herself upstairs, she had one thing to do before visiting the delectable Dr Carter. She bent forward enough to catch herself in the mirror, and applied blush to her cheeks and ran the brush through her locks. Her bright eyes reflected back at her, *'steady your nerves, Hetty,'* she whispered. With one final look in the oval mirror, she gathered her skirts and hurried down the stairs.

"Hetty? Where are you? I expected you to leave ten minutes ago!"

"I'm going now, Father."

"Hetty?"

She turned around before stepping out of the front door.

"I can see what you have done to your face, I am no fool."

Hetty caught her breath and bit her top lip. "That obvious, is it?"

Thomas smiled back at his only child. "You don't need it, you are beautiful enough without that muck on your face. And don't be long, my dear, you are needed here, not in Dr Carter's office. You're merely there to borrow some arsenic for our preservation work. Nothing more, nothing less."

Hetty nodded once before hurrying out of the door. Her slender fingers trembled slightly as she reached for the polished brass handle of the carriage door. The vehicle, a sombre relic with soot clinging to its once lustrous surface, creaked mournfully as she pulled it open.

She ascended the carriage steps with a grace that seemed at odds with the somber facade of the undertaker's shop behind her. As the wheels began to turn, carrying her towards Dr Carter's office, Hetty couldn't help but reflect on how quickly fortunes could change—how the unexpected loss of her mother had set in motion a chain of events that now required her to undertake such an errand.

The carriage rolled on, a relic of past affluence now serving a far more pragmatic—and precarious—purpose.

She steadied her breath, her eyes fixed on the small leather pouch nestled in her lap. It was more than mere fabric and coin; it was the embodiment of her family's precarious existence.

Hetty looked out of the window and wrapped her shawl tighter against the chill as they trundled along, the sickly-sweet scent of decay mingling with the pervasive smog.

As the carriage rolled to a halt outside the physician's office, Hetty took a deep breath, steeling herself for the task ahead. *'Remember,'* she whispered, echoing her father's instructions, *'you're merely there to borrow some arsenic for our... preservation work. Nothing more, nothing less.'*

Her hand tightened around the leather pouch, its contents a grim reminder of the precarious line they walked between life and death, legality and desperation.

As Hetty stepped down from the carriage, she squared her shoulders, ready to face whatever lay beyond the physician's door. And with each step, she imagined falling into Dr Carter's arms and being saved from the torrid life she detested that existed inside the walls of her father's undertaker's parlour.

Hetty Morgan lifted the hem of her dark blue gown as she approached the physician's office, her gaze catching on a burst of colour that seemed out of place in the drab world of death. The small garden at the front of the building, vibrant with flowers in full bloom, beckoned her weary eyes. Roses, daffodils, and lilacs thrived within the wrought-iron fence, their petals swaying gently in the cool breeze.

'Such beauty in a place of science,' Hetty murmured to herself, allowing a momentary respite from her burdensome thoughts. The flowers, so full of life and vibrancy, stood in stark contrast to the work she carried out, offering a silent promise of hope she scarcely dared to grasp.

Taking a deep breath, she stepped through the door, the bell above chiming its announcement of her arrival. The interior of Mr George Carter's office was a sanctuary of calm, lined with books and medical instruments that spoke of his dedication to healing.

"Miss Morgan," came a voice, smooth and reassuring like a balm to her frayed nerves.

Hetty's gaze lifted, and she found herself locking eyes with the physician himself. His tall frame was poised with an innate confidence, yet it was his warm eyes, glimmering with genuine kindness, which drew her in. An honest smile curved his lips, touching his eyes in a way that made her heart skip a beat and the tiny hairs on the backs of her hands stand on end.

"Dr Carter," she greeted, her voice steadier than she felt. "I trust the morning finds you well?"

"Indeed, it does, Miss Morgan," he replied, stepping closer. "Though I must say, your presence here brings a light to this solemn day."

"Light?" She couldn't help the flicker of surprise that danced across her face. "I carry naught but shadows, Sir."

"Ah, but even the darkest shadows are cast by the brightest lights," he said, a playful edge to his words. "And I dare say, the flowers outside seem to agree. They brighten considerably in your presence."

Hetty felt a warmth spread through her chest, a feeling that was both alien and exhilarating. She allowed herself a small, genuine smile—one that reached her eyes for the first time in what felt like an eternity.

"Flowers are easily charmed, Dr Carter," she quipped back, finding solace in the easy banter. "But I am afraid I cannot linger too long to test your theory. I have come to borrow some arsenic, Father sent me. He told me not to take any longer than required, duty calls, as you well know."

"Of course," he acknowledged with a nod, the light in his eyes dimming slightly at the thought of Hetty Morgan leaving so soon. "Duty is an unforgiving master. But perhaps, one day, you'll allow yourself some leisure to prove my little hypothesis about the flowers."

"Perhaps," Hetty conceded, the word hanging between them like a delicate promise, tethered to dreams of a different life—a life where hope was more than just a fleeting visitor in her heart.

"Miss Morgan," Dr Carter began, his voice a soothing balm to the harshness of her day, "I must commend you on your fortitude. Not many could manage such tasks with the grace you exhibit."

Hetty felt the weight of his gaze, as if he were peering into the very essence of her being. She arranged her features into a mask of poise, though her hands trembled slightly against the fabric of her skirt. "It is not a matter of choice, Dr Carter," she replied evenly. "One does what one must for family."

"Indeed." He nodded, the thoughtful brown of his eyes darkening with something that resembled respect. "Yet, it speaks volumes of your character. These are trying times for Blackstone."

The mention of their grim surroundings drew a line between them, an unspoken acknowledgment of the darkness that had recently befallen their town.

"Trying times indeed," Hetty echoed, her voice barely above a whisper. "The recent murders have everyone on edge."

"Ah, yes, the unfortunate business with the killings," he said, leaning forward slightly, his expression solemn. "A blight upon our streets. It seems no one is safe these days."

"Indeed," Hetty agreed, her heart quickening. "It's disconcerting, how close to home such violence has come."

"Your concern is understandable," he replied, his gaze never wavering from hers. "It takes a strong will to face such fears head-on, as you do."

"Thank you, Sir. But it is not only for myself that I worry." Her voice trailed off, the implication hanging heavily between them.

"Of course," George murmured, acknowledging the gravity of her unspoken words. "The safety of one's family is paramount."

"Exactly so," she said, feeling the weight of his admiration like a mantle upon her shoulders. "I fear for what these times will bring next."

"Rest assured, Miss Morgan," he promised, a steadfast determination in his tone, "I am committed to doing all I can to aid this community and put an end to this senseless violence. We shall see justice done."

As Hetty turned away from the window, she took a silent moment to anchor herself in the small haven of warmth and security that Dr Carter's office provided.

"Tell me, Miss Morgan," George said, leaning against his polished mahogany desk, his eyes reflecting a genuine interest that was rare in Hetty's world, "what dreams do you harbour within that resilient heart of yours?"

She hesitated, unaccustomed to such inquiries about her own desires. "Dreams, Dr Carter, are luxuries afforded to those not bound by certain obligations." Her eyes flickered away momentarily before finding courage to meet his gaze once more. "But if I dare to dream, it would be for a life graced with dignity. To walk down the street without whispers trailing behind me."

"Ah," he nodded thoughtfully. "And perhaps one day, those whispers will turn into admiration for the woman who overcame adversities most cannot fathom."

"Perhaps," she whispered, allowing herself a sliver of hope.

His smile was encouraging, and he moved subtly closer. "As for myself, I dream of advancing medicine. To bring healing where there is hurt, knowledge where there is ignorance."

"Such noble aspirations, Dr Carter," Hetty replied, her voice laced with genuine awe. She found herself drawn to his fervour, to the passion that animated his features. "It seems we both seek to transform our corner of the world, however daunting the task."

"Indeed, we do," he agreed, their shared laughter briefly intertwining their spirits.

In that moment, as they stood merely a whisper apart, Hetty felt an exhilarating connection. The room—with its medical texts and the gentle flicker of gaslight—seemed to recede until there was only the man before her, whose presence sparked a sense of belonging she'd never known. It was a feeling so potent, so intoxicating, that for a heartbeat, she forgot the shadows that clung to her name.

"Miss Morgan," George began, his voice low and compelling, "your resilience is a beacon in this dreary place. You make me believe that change is possible, even here."

"Dr Carter," Hetty responded, her breath catching, "you give me hope that there might be a place for me beyond the confines of duty and despair."

Their eyes locked, and the air between them crackled with the promise of what could be. Hetty felt torn, caught between the burgeoning pull towards this man who saw her for who she truly was and the dark legacy that bound her to silence and sacrifice.

"Hope is a powerful force, Miss Morgan," George murmured, his thumb brushing ever so lightly against the back of her hand—a touch scandalous in its intimacy yet tender in its restraint.

"Indeed, it is," she breathed, feeling the stirrings of something deep within—a yearning for life beyond the burdens she carried.

The sharp rapping on the door shattered the fragile cocoon they had woven around themselves. The sound was insistent, urgent—a harbinger of reality impatiently demanding entry.

Hetty's hand instinctively tightened on the edge of her skirt, her knuckles whitening as she straightened, drawing upon her well of composure. "Duty calls," she said, a tinge of melancholy lacing her words.

George's brow furrowed, his frame tensing as he moved towards the door, "One moment, Miss Morgan." He opened it to reveal his assistant, whose face was ashen, eyes wide with alarm.

"Dr Carter, Sir," the young man stammered, "there's been another one... another murder."

A chill swept through the room, snuffing out the warmth of their prior exchange. George's expression darkened, the genial lines of his face giving way to the stern contours of resolve. "I understand," he replied curtly. "Thank you, Billy. Please ensure the constable knows I'm available for consultation."

"Of course, Sir," Billy replied, nodding briskly before retreating, leaving them once again alone.

"Another murder?" Hetty echoed, her heart racing with a mix of fear and the grim familiarity of death that seemed an ever-present shadow in Blackstone.

"Indeed," George said, his gaze locking with hers. "This scourge upon our district must be stopped. I've seen enough of death, Miss Morgan. It's time for justice to prevail."

"Justice," Hetty repeated softly, her admiration for the man before her swelling like a tide. "You wish to be part of the solution then?"

"More than anything," he affirmed, "I am committed to this community, to its healing. We cannot let darkness reign unchecked."

"Nor shall we," Hetty stated, feeling a surge of solidarity. "Your dedication, Dr Carter, it's..." She paused, searching for the word that would encapsulate the swell of respect she felt.

"Admirable?" he offered, a rueful half-smile touching his lips.

"Yes, admirable," she agreed, the corners of her own mouth lifting despite the recent news. "And inspiring."

"Then let us draw inspiration from each other," George suggested. He moved to the door, the messenger's shadow retreating down the hallway. His back was a line of steadiness, the set of his shoulders speaking of burdens willingly shouldered.

Hetty watched him, her chest tight with an emotion she dared not name.

"Miss Morgan," George said, turning back toward her, his voice carrying the weight of their interrupted moment. "I must attend to this dreadful business, but I—"

"Please, Dr Carter, there's no need for apologies." Her words were hushed, an attempt to veil the disappointment that threatened to spill over. But as their eyes met once more, words became unnecessary.

"Hetty," George began, hesitating as her name hung tenderly on his lips, a privilege she felt deep in her bones. "Be safe," he added, the concern in his gaze wrapping around her like a warm shawl.

"Always, Dr Carter," she replied, offering him the same silent vow.

The carriage wheels crunched over the cobblestones, jostling Hetty as she leaned back against the worn leather seat. Her hands clasped tightly in her lap, betraying an inner turmoil that belied her composed exterior.

The rhythmic trot of the horse and the distant echo of street vendors gradually faded beneath the clamour of her thoughts.

"Miss Morgan?" The driver's voice broke through her reverie. "We're nearing your residence."

"Thank you, Mr Hawkins," she replied, her gaze fixed on the passing scenery—slum houses, street sellers, and costermongers. Nothing but hardship and struggle. A sight that would stay with her for life.

"Forgive me for pryin', but you seem different," Mr Hawkins ventured, casting a glance over his shoulder.

Hetty offered a faint smile, her eyes still lost to the night. "I suppose even the darkest of duties can yield unexpected encounters."

"Ah, life's full o' surprises, it is," Mr Hawkins agreed with a knowing nod, leaving her to retreat once more into her private world of thoughts.

Meanwhile, inside the physician's office, George Carter lingered by the window, watching the carriage disappear into the gloom of Blackstone's streets. He turned to his assistant; his brow creased with contemplation.

"Billy, did you notice Miss Morgan's demeanour? There's something remarkable about her resolve."

"Indeed, Sir," Billy agreed, adjusting his spectacles. "She carries herself with a grace uncommon in our line of work."

"Grace." George mused. "Yes, that's precisely it. And yet there's a fire in her, a quiet strength that draws one in." He paced the room, hands clasped behind his back. "Do you believe in fate, Billy?"

"Sometimes, Sir," Billy responded, stacking papers on the desk. "Though often, it seems more like chance playing its hand."

"Perhaps," George conceded, the image of Hetty's piercing blue eyes etched in his mind. "But there are times when two paths cross, and one cannot help but wonder if there's a purpose behind it all."

"Only time will tell, Dr Carter," Billy said sagely, offering a small smile.

"Yes," George whispered, his heart quickening at the prospect. "Time will indeed tell."

Chapter Four

Grace Pembroke stood concealed behind the heavy drapery of her parlour window, her gaze fixed on the fading silhouette of Miss Hetty Morgan's carriage as it rumbled down the street. The rhythmic clatter of the horses' hooves echoed in the distance, yet it was not the sound that drew Grace's focus but the sight of George Carter at his window, lost in thought.

'Always so pensive, my dear George,' she murmured to herself, a touch of mockery lacing her words.

Her heart had fluttered with an uncharacteristic unease when she'd witnessed the silent, yet tender exchange between Hetty and George. It was a mere moment, fleeting and perhaps inconsequential to any other observer, but not to Grace. For she did not have to hear the words spoken between her future fiancé and undertaker's lass, to know that trouble was ahead.

"Hetty Morgan, of all people," Grace scoffed quietly, her fingers tightening around the luxurious fabric of the curtains. "A common undertaker's daughter."

As the last echo of the carriage faded, she released the drapery and turned away from the window. Her reflection in the mirror caught her eye—poise and grace personified. Yet, beneath the surface, a storm brewed.

"Miss Pembroke, shall I see to your evening tea?" the voice of her lady's maid interrupted her reverie.

"Leave it, Annabelle," Grace responded sharply, dismissing the maid with a wave of her hand. She needed no comfort of chamomile or the solace of solitude; she required strategy.

'*George cannot be so easily swayed by simple sentimentality,*' she reasoned aloud, pacing the length of the room. '*He is a man of stature, of science. He needs a partner who can match him, not drag him down with provincial notions and morbid family affairs.*'

In her mind's eye, the pieces of her social chess board began to shift. Grace knew the rules of high society's game better than most, and she intended to play to win.

"Annabelle," Grace called out, halting her pacing. The maid reappeared promptly, a look of apprehension on her face.

"Send word to Lady Henley. Tell her I wish to call upon her tomorrow morning," Grace instructed, her tone now composed and authoritative.

"Very good, Miss Pembroke," Annabelle replied, curtsying before withdrawing to carry out the task.

Grace mused to herself, a calculating glint in her eyes. '*The perfect setting for a most enlightening conversation about the dangers lurking in Blackstone... and the unsuitability of certain individuals.*'

Grace settled into an armchair, smoothing the folds of her dress as she considered her next move. '*Poor George,*' she sighed theatrically, though no one was present to hear her feigned sympathy. '*He must be protected from such... undesirable influences.*'

With a final glance towards the street where Hetty's carriage had vanished, Grace Pembroke's expression hardened. In her world, there was no room for rivals—not when the stakes were this high. She would act swiftly, decisively, and without remorse. After all, this was more than a matter of the heart; it was a battle for status, for security, and for a future she believed rightfully hers.

'*Hetty Morgan will learn her place,*' Grace whispered, the words a silent vow. '*And George will remain mine.*'

Chapter Five

The flickering gaslight cast long shadows across the morgue as Hetty Morgan carefully recorded the details of their latest arrival. Her quill scratched softly against the ledger, the sound mingling with the ticking of the old clock on the wall. But even as her hand moved mechanically across the page, her mind was elsewhere, caught in a web of suspicion and unease.

Mr Grayson's recent visit to her father had stirred something within her. The hushed tones, the furtive glances, the palpable tension that had lingered in the air long after the coroner's departure – all of it gnawed at her conscience, demanding attention.

"Hetty?" Her father's voice startled her from her reverie. "Have you finished with Mr Holloway's entry?"

She looked up, meeting Thomas Morgan's weary gaze. "Almost, Father. Just a few more details to note."

He nodded, his eyes darting away quickly – too quickly. It was a small thing, perhaps, but it didn't escape Hetty's notice. Lately, every interaction with her father seemed laden with unspoken words and hidden meanings.

As Thomas retreated to his office, Hetty's gaze fell upon the body of Mr Holloway. There was something off about his arrival. The usual documentation was sparse, the details of his passing vague at best. It wasn't the first time she'd noticed such discrepancies in recent weeks.

With a furtive glance towards her father's closed door, Hetty quickly jotted down her observations in a small notebook she'd taken to keeping on her person. It was a risk, she knew, but one she felt compelled to take.

Later that evening, after her father had retired for the night, Hetty slipped out into the cool air. The streets were quiet, save for the distant sounds of a drunk's warbling song and the occasional rattle of a passing carriage.

Her destination was The Crow and Crown, a tavern frequented by the working class. It wasn't a place a young lady should be seen, but Hetty had long since learned that propriety often stood in the way of truth.

"Evening, Miss Morgan," the barkeep greeted her with a nod as she entered. "Usual spot?"

Hetty smiled tightly, making her way to a secluded corner where a hunched figure awaited her.

"Mr Finch," she said softly, sliding into the seat across from the elderly gravedigger. "I trust you have some information for me?"

Jeremiah Finch looked up, his rheumy eyes darting nervously around the pub before settling on Hetty. "Aye, Miss. Though I don't know how much good it'll do ye. Strange goings-on at the cemetery, there are. Bodies going missing, new ones arriving with nary a word of explanation."

Hetty leaned in, her heart quickening. "And the most recent? Mr Holloway?"

Finch's wrinkled face contorted in a grimace. "Never saw him arrive, Miss. Just found him in the morgue one mornin', like he'd appeared out of thin air."

A chill ran down Hetty's spine. It confirmed her suspicions – something was very wrong in Blackstone, and somehow, her father was involved.

As she made her way home that night, Hetty's mind raced. The pieces were there, but they refused to form a clear picture. The increased number of bodies, her father's nervous behavior, Mr Grayson's clandestine visits – what did it all mean?

She thought of Dr Carter, of the warmth in his eyes and the strength in his convictions. Would he believe her if she shared her suspicions? Or would he, like so many others, dismiss her as a morbid undertaker's daughter with an overactive imagination?

Hetty paused at the corner of Willow Street, her gaze drawn to a modest terraced house. She'd heard whispers about the Pritchards – about how Archibald Pritchard had been asking questions before his untimely death. Perhaps his wife and son would understand her concerns if she spoke to them.

With a deep breath, Hetty steeled herself for what lay ahead. She knew that pursuing this matter further would be dangerous, that it could upend her life and the lives of those she cared about. But she also knew that she couldn't turn back now. The truth, no matter how ugly, had to be brought to light.

As she turned towards home, Hetty was unaware of the eyes watching her – eyes that had noted her meeting in the tavern and followed her journey through the darkened streets of the grim town.

Chapter Six

The house on Willow Street stood in stark contrast to the grander homes on the outskirts of Blackstone that had grounds, gardens, and rose lined driveways. Its red brick facade, weathered by years of sun and rain, spoke of a quiet dignity that matched its occupants perfectly.

Inside, Beatrice Pritchard moved about the cozy sitting room, dusting shelves lined with well-worn books and mementos of a life well-lived. Her son, Frederick, sat by the window, ostensibly reading the morning paper but his eyes kept drifting to the street outside.

"You're fretting again, Frederick," Beatrice said softly, pausing in her work to regard her son with a mixture of concern and affection.

Frederick sighed, folding the paper, and setting it aside. "Can you blame me, Ma? The whispers in town, they're getting louder. People are talking about Hetty Morgan, about her asking questions, poking into matters that no other man or woman dare to."

Beatrice's hands stilled on the mantelpiece, her eyes growing distant. "She's not in the papers is she? Who would report on that?"

"No, Ma. I've heard the gossip in the town."

"It's about time someone did ask questions. They should have been asked when Archibald was brutally taken from us. Then perhaps there would have been fewer suspicious deaths."

The unspoken presence of Archibald Pritchard, Beatrice's husband and Frederick's father, seemed to fill the room. Though it had been two years since his murder, the pain of his loss was still a tangible thing, as real as the faded photograph that held pride of place on the mantel.

"You're right, Ma. The resurrectionists were behind Pa's death. There was no other explanation." Frederick said, voicing the subject that had haunted them both for so long.

Beatrice turned to face her son, her usually gentle features hardening with resolve. "It's only because your father was getting too close to the truth that they had no choice but to kill him. He asked too many questions about the bodies going missing from the cemetery. And then, suddenly..." Her voice trailed off, choked with emotion.

Frederick rose, crossing the room to embrace his mother. "I know, Ma. I miss him too."

As they held each other, the painful memories of that fateful night two years ago came flooding back. Archibald had been found at the bottom of a deep, freshly dug grave in the cemetery, his body broken and lifeless. Mr Grayson, the local coroner, had swiftly declared it a tragic accident – a fall in the dark – but the Pritchards knew better.

The telltale signs had been there, subtle yet damning to those who truly looked. Archibald's coat pocket had been torn, as if something had been hastily removed. A faint, sweet odour clung to his clothes, reminiscent of the ether used in hospitals – an odd scent to find in a graveyard. The missing signet ring, a family heirloom Archibald never removed, was suspiciously absent from his finger - surely that wouldn't have slipped off when he fell?

But there was more, details that haunted Frederick's dreams. The pocket watch, always wound precisely, had stopped at 11:47 pm – far too early for Archibald's bedtime. Dark smudges on his father's shirt cuffs and collar spoke of recent writing, likely the damning evidence that had sealed his fate.

Most chilling of all was the small mark on Archibald's neck, easily dismissed as a scratch from the fall. But Frederick couldn't shake the memory of the time he'd accompanied his father to visit a sick patient.

He'd watched, fascinated, as the doctor had used a strange needle to inject medicine directly into the man's neck, leaving a similar mark. The thought that someone might have done the same to his father, not to heal but to harm, made Frederick's blood run cold.

"Mr Grayson insisted it was an accident," Beatrice whispered, her voice thick with grief and anger. "He said Archibald must have been checking on a recent burial and lost his footing in the dark. But we knew better. Even Constable Mills looked doubtful, though he daren't speak against the verdict after what happened to your father."

Frederick nodded grimly. "Pa was getting too close. He'd traced the pattern of grave robberies, started connecting them to mysterious deaths around town. The resurrectionists couldn't risk him exposing their operation."

"Your father always said that evil thrives in silence," Beatrice murmured, pulling back to look at her son with tears in her eyes. "He gave his life trying to break that silence."

Frederick's jaw tightened. "And we won't let his sacrifice be in vain. Somehow, we'll find a way to finish what he started."

As they stood there, drawing comfort from each other's presence, a commotion outside drew their attention. They moved to the window, watching as Hetty Morgan hurried down the street, her face set with determination.

"She's brave, that one," Beatrice said, a note of admiration in her voice. "Reminds me of your father."

Frederick nodded slowly, a decision crystallising in his mind. "Perhaps we should offer our help. We have Father's notes, his suspicions. They might be useful to her investigation."

Beatrice looked at her son, seeing in him the same courage and sense of justice that had defined Archibald. "It would be dangerous," she warned, though there was no real objection in her tone.

"So was Pa's work," Frederick countered. "But he believed in doing what was right, no matter the cost. Don't we owe it to him to see this through?"

A long moment passed as Beatrice considered her son's words. Finally, she nodded, a small smile tugging at the corners of her mouth. "Your father would be proud of you, Frederick. And you're right. It's time we stopped hiding from the truth and started fighting for it."

As the afternoon light began to fade, Beatrice and Frederick sat at the kitchen table, surrounded by Archibald's old papers and notebooks. The gravity of what they had uncovered weighed heavily upon them.

"We can't keep this to ourselves any longer," Frederick said, his voice low but determined. "We need to meet Hetty face to face. She needs to know what Pa suspected, the connections he was beginning to make before he passed."

Beatrice nodded, her eyes bright with unshed tears. "You're right. Your father always said that the truth has a way of coming to light, no matter how deep it's buried. Perhaps this is our chance to help that process along."

Frederick stood; decision made. "I'll go to her tomorrow. We'll offer our help, share what we know. It's what Father would have wanted."

Beatrice stood, decision made. "We must be careful, my dear," Beatrice cautioned, reaching out to squeeze her son's hand. "The forces at work here are powerful and dangerous. They've already taken your father from us. I couldn't bear to lose you too."

Frederick's expression softened as he looked at his mother. "I promise we will be cautious, Ma. But we can't stand idly by, not when we have the chance to make a difference."

"Then I will arrange to meet with Hetty, she is likely to trust a woman more than a young man." As night fell over Blackstone, the Pritchards prepared themselves for what was to come. They knew that by aligning themselves with Hetty Morgan, they were stepping into a world of danger and intrigue. But they also knew that it was the right thing to do, the only way to honour Archibald's memory and perhaps, finally, bring his killers to justice.

Chapter Seven

George Carter stood at the window of his study, gazing out at the manicured gardens of the Carter estate without really seeing them. His mind was a whirlwind of conflicting thoughts and emotions, each vying for dominance in the turmoil of his heart.

The weight of the engagement ring in his pocket seemed to grow heavier with each passing moment. Grace Pembroke was everything a man of his station could want in a wife – beautiful, well-connected, and impeccably bred. Their union would cement the Carter family's position in society and open doors to even greater influence and wealth.

And yet, the image of Hetty Morgan's face swam before his mind's eye, her face alight with intelligence and passion. In the few brief encounters they had shared, George had felt more alive than in all his years of navigating the carefully choreographed dance of high society.

A soft knock at the door interrupted his reverie. "Come in," he called, turning from the window.

His brother, Robert, entered, a look of concern creasing his brow. "George, Father's asking for you. Something about finalising the details of the engagement announcement."

George suppressed a sigh, nodding tersely. "I'll be there shortly."

Robert lingered, studying his younger brother's face. "Is everything alright, George? You seem distracted lately."

For a moment, George considered confiding in Robert, sharing the doubts that plagued him. But the words died on his lips. How could he explain something he scarcely understood himself?

"It's nothing," he said finally, forcing a smile. "Just wedding jitters, I suppose."

Robert looked unconvinced but didn't press the issue. As he turned to leave, he paused at the door. "You know, George, it's not too late to change your mind. If you're having doubts, then you need to say something. Do something. You can't live a life full of regret just to open more doors for the family."

"And disappoint Father? Throw away years of planning?" George shook his head. "No, the course is set. I'll do my duty, as any Carter should."

After Robert left, George returned to the window, his gaze drawn inexorably to the distant rooftops of the town. Somewhere out there, Hetty Morgan was going about her day, unaware of the turmoil she had sparked in his heart.

What was it about her that called to him so strongly? Her courage in the face of adversity? The quiet strength that seemed to radiate from her very being? Or perhaps it was the glimpse of a life lived with purpose, so different from the gilded cage of his own existence.

George's hand clenched around the ring in his pocket. He had a choice to make, one that would shape his future. The easy path lay before him – marriage to Grace, a life of privilege and comfort. But was that truly what he wanted?

As he turned to answer his father's summons, George felt a resolve hardening within him. He would honour his engagement to Grace, play the part that was expected of him. But he would also seek out Hetty Morgan, if only to understand the strange pull she exerted on his heart.

Chapter Eight

Hetty Morgan's fingers trembled slightly as she sliced through the loaf of bread, each cut a jagged echo of the fluttering in her heart. She paused, closing her eyes to savour the memory that had been playing on a loop in her mind — Dr George Carter's smile, warm and inviting like a hearth in winter.

'*Such a gentleman,*' she murmured to herself, a faint blush colouring her cheeks. The candlelight flickered, casting dancing shadows across the walls of the kitchen, a stark contrast to the light his presence had brought into her life, if only for a moment.

"Stew again?" Her father's voice cut through the quiet, gruff and weary from the day's work, as he entered the room. He lifted his nose, closed his eyes, and breathed in the hearty scent and aroma of the pig trotters and broth wafting high above the pot. "Ah, well, it fills the belly."

"Father, you know we must make do with what we have," Hetty replied, not turning to face him as she busied herself with stirring the pot hanging over their modest fireplace.

"Indeed." His sigh was almost lost amid the clatter of cutlery as he set the table.

The window hung open a crack, an attempt to dispel the scent of boiling pig trotters, but instead, it allowed the pervasive scent of burnt coal to drift in from the streets. It mingled unpleasantly with the underlying odour of decay that never quite left the air, emanating from Thomas Morgan's parlour below — the harsh reality of his profession as an undertaker.

"Can you smell that, Father?" Hetty asked quietly, her voice laced with yearning. "The soot, the smoke, it's everywhere. It sticks to the skin."

Thomas Morgan glanced at his daughter, noting the longing in her gaze as she looked out towards the window. "It's the smell of hard work, Hetty. The smell of life here."

"Is it foolish to wish for a life less grim?" she ventured, her eyes meeting his, revealing a depth of sorrow and hope.

"Hope can be a dangerous thing," he replied, his voice softening. "But no, child, it is not foolish."

"Dr Carter spoke about the world beyond Blackstone, about places where the air is clean and the grass is green," Hetty said, her voice barely above a whisper, as if afraid to shatter the delicate web of her dreams.

"Dr Carter has the luxury of such thoughts," her father countered, though not unkindly. "We must live in the world as it is."

"Perhaps," Hetty conceded, but her heart rebelled silently against the notion. She couldn't help but cling to the vision of a different life, one touched by the kindness reflected in George Carter's eyes.

"Let us eat," Thomas finally said, motioning to the simple meal before them. And they did, in companionable silence, punctuated only by the clinking of spoons against bowls and the distant murmur of Blackstone settling into the twilight hours.

Hetty Morgan sat by the narrow window of her father's home, her fingers tracing idle patterns on the foggy pane. She could still hear her father's words, their meaning sinking into the marrow of her bones. In the quiet, the sound of her own heartbeat seemed loud, each thump a reminder of what might be—what should be—beyond these walls.

'*Hope can be a dangerous thing,*' her father had said.

But wasn't hope also the ember that warmed the cold nights? The light that led one through the dark?

"Hetty," her father called from the adjoining room, his voice tinged with a secrecy that always followed him like a shadow.

"Yes?" she responded, turning her gaze from the mist-laden view outside.

"Come help me with something," he beckoned, his figure obscured by the doorway leading down to his workshop.

She rose, her limbs heavy with reluctance. Stepping into the workshop, she was met with the familiar scent of chemicals and the sight of medical texts strewn across the table. Her father's dealings were never spoken outright, yet the rumours that seeped through the cracks of their home spoke volumes.

"Be careful with that," Thomas instructed as he handed her a small vial. "It's for preserving specimens. Let's finish this," he said.

"What do you need me to do?"

"Tidy up these shelves, we are set for a busy week with three bodies arriving first thing."

"Three?" Hetty said, raising her eyebrows. "That's more than normal. What's causing the deaths? I don't think there is an outbreak of Cholera at the moment."

"It doesn't matter what's causing them. It is merely our job to dress and clean the bodies, so they are ready for ..."

"Ready for what, father?"

"Their onward journey, wherever that may be!" He shouted.

Hetty looked away with pink, mottled cheeks.

Thomas noticed her sadness from the way he had shouted at her. There was no malice intended, it was just that he had a lot of secrets that he didn't wish for his daughter to know. "I'm sorry, Hetty. I didn't mean to shout."

Hetty smiled, meekly. "You are forgiven, but you must promise me this. If you have engaged in something that is criminal, then it must be shared with me so I can help."

"Criminal? Well, I never would. It's not worth risking my job over, we need the money."

"Indeed we do. Just make sure the money is earned from genuine sources and not criminal ways."

"You would do well with just getting on with what I have asked, not questioning me."

"Very well," she responded.

Hetty continued straightening the jars of liquid that would be used on the dead. She knew her father was involved in the murders, she just didn't want to believe it.

Questions would be asked, and enquiries made, if only to clear her father's name.

Chapter Nine

Grace Pembroke's heels clicked decisively against the cobblestones as she navigated the bustling streets. The murmur of the marketplace buzzed around her, a symphony of haggling voices and the clatter of carts. Her green eyes, sharp as cut emeralds, swept over the scene with measured indifference until fragments of a conversation snagged her attention like the thorns of a bramble.

"Have you seen the way Dr Carter looks at Miss Morgan?" A woman's voice floated on the air, ripe with insinuation.

"Indeed," another chimed in, "such attention from a man of his standing is most unusual."

THE DAUGHTER'S ENDURING LOVE

"Most promising, if you ask me," the first replied with a titter.

Grace felt the words coil around her heart like a serpent. She drew closer, the whispers painting an image she wished to tear to shreds. The thought of George Carter, her betrothed, casting glances at Hetty Morgan stoked a fire within her, and Grace knew it was a blaze she must smother.

"Unusual and entirely misplaced," Grace interjected smoothly, her tone laced with a frost that belied the polite smile on her lips. "One must not mistake politeness for affection, ladies."

The women turned, their faces blooming with surprise and embarrassment upon recognising Miss Pembroke. They murmured apologies, but Grace paid them no mind, her thoughts were already weaving a tapestry of obstruction, her jealousy the needle pulling the thread tight.

Grace arrived at her friend's home and was met by the butler. "Lady Henley is expecting you, follow me."

Grace nodded once and silently followed him to the drawing room.

"Darlings," Grace Pembroke's voice dripped with a sweet poison, "have you heard the latest whispers about Miss Hetty Morgan?" She looked around at each of the ladies who had been waiting with eager anticipation for Grace's news.

Her friends, gathered around her in the opulence of the Henley's drawing room, leaned in closer. Teacups paused mid-sip, eyes wide with anticipation.

"Whatever do you mean, Grace?" cooed Harriet, her own curiosity piqued by the promise of scandalous gossip.

Grace flicked an imaginary speck of dust from her pristine dress and sighed dramatically. "It pains me to say, but it seems some people lack the decency that befits our station. Miss Morgan, for instance," she lowered her voice, ensuring every ear was attuned to her words alone, "seems intent on climbing above her lowly station, ensnaring those who are unwary."

"Surely not George Carter!" Constance gasped, her hand fluttering to her throat.

"George is far too kind, too charitable," Grace said, imbuing the word with disdain. "But we must consider the company Miss Morgan keeps. Her father's workshop, the odious stench, the rumours of unsavoury dealings." She let the implication hang heavy in the air.

"Goodness, you mean the resurrectionists?" whispered Margaret, her face blanching.

"Indeed," Grace affirmed with a solemn nod. "One cannot be too careful with whom one associates, especially with such vile rumours afoot. It would be most unfortunate if George were to be entangled in such a web. Especially since news of the murders lead back to Hetty Morgan's father."

"Most unfortunate," echoed her friends in agreement.

"Then it's settled," Grace concluded with finality. "We shall ensure that Dr Carter remains unblemished by such scandal. It is our duty, after all."

With nods of assent, the ladies rose, their mission clear as they filed out of the drawing room, each now a carrier of the poison seed Grace had so carefully planted.

Chapter Ten

⁕

The marketplace of Blackstone buzzed with the energy of commerce, the cacophony of hawkers and housewives bartering under the smoggy sky. But beneath the din, another currency traded hands – that of whispers and pointed fingers.

"Have you heard?" The question passed from vendor to buyer, from fishmonger to maid.

"About the Morgans? That poor Dr Carter..."

"Such a shame, really. A gentleman like him, caught up with that sort..."

"Her father, they say, deals with the dead more than the living..."

"Grave robbers, all of them! And she's trying to snare a good man! Does he know her father is a murderer?"

The murmurs swirled, becoming as much a part of the market's fabric as the stalls themselves. Suspicion cast long shadows over the cobbled streets, mixing with the tangible fear of the resurrectionist gang that haunted the nightmares of the town's residents.

"Hetty Morgan," spat a matronly woman, buying a loaf of bread. "Mark my words, she'll be the ruin of that fine young man. No good can come from fraternising with that sort."

"Indeed," agreed the baker, handing over the bread with a grave nod. "A pity about her and George Carter. He'd do well to listen to Miss Pembroke. She knows what's best for him."

"Miss Pembroke," the woman repeated, tucking the bread under her arm. "She's got her head on straight, that one. She'll keep him safe from the likes of Hetty Morgan."

Hetty clenched her fingers around the basket handle, her knuckles blanching as she navigated through Blackstone's crowded market. The weight of whispers followed her, each glance and nudge from the townsfolk a silent confirmation of Grace Pembroke's poison dripping through their minds.

"Miss Morgan," a familiar voice cut through the hum of bartering voices and clinking coins, its gentle timbre a stark contrast to the cacophony of suspicion.

"Dr Carter," Hetty greeted, her tone guarded yet tinged with a warmth she couldn't suppress. George stood before her, his eyes meeting hers with an intensity that seemed to push away the din and dirt of the marketplace.

"May I accompany you?" he asked, his gaze never wavering despite the risk their proximity posed to both their reputations.

"Would it not be unseemly, Sir? Have you not heard the whispers and gossip?" Hetty glanced around, acutely aware of the eyes that trailed over them with mounting interest.

"Perhaps," George admitted. "But I find myself increasingly indifferent to such concerns."

They walked side by side in silence for a moment, the space between them charged with a connection neither could openly acknowledge. Hetty's heart raced; George was betrothed to another, yet here he was, challenging convention with his mere presence at her side.

"Miss Morgan," George began, his voice low, "I fear the expectations placed upon me are like chains. My impending engagement to Miss Pembroke ..." He hesitated, searching her face for understanding. "It is not where my heart lies."

Hetty felt her breath catch, her pulse quickening as she dared to hope. "Society can be a cruel jailer," she murmured, her words carefully chosen yet laced with the vulnerability she felt. "We're all prisoners in some manner."

"Indeed," George agreed, his gaze turning inward. "Yet when I am with you, I sense a possibility of freedom, a chance to—"

"To live as we truly are," Hetty finished for him, her blue eyes reflecting the very notion that haunted her dreams.

"Exactly so," he said, the corner of his mouth lifting in a brief, genuine smile that seemed to light up the grim surroundings.

Their shared understanding was a fragile bubble which was threatened by the swirling eddies of rumour and obligation. Yet for that fleeting moment, as they walked together amidst the chaos, Hetty and George found solace in their silent rebellion against the world's expectations.

At the end of the street, hidden within the shadow of a draping willow, Miss Grace Pembroke's gaze lingered upon Hetty and George as they parted ways. The corners of her mouth curved into a semblance of sweetness, an artful disguise for the venom coiling in her heart. She watched them with the precision of a hawk, each flutter of her eyelids calculating the gravity of the threat that Hetty posed.

'*Hetty Morgan,*' Grace whispered to herself, a promise etched into each syllable. '*You shall not ensnare him. Not while I draw breath.*'

With the stealth of a cat, she retreated into the labyrinth of alleyways, where the tang of river mist mingled with the acrid smoke from nearby factories. Her mind was abuzz with schemes, each more cunning than the last.

Chapter Eleven

The following morning found Hetty at the local bakery, the warm aroma of fresh bread offering little solace from the chill of confrontation as she noticed Grace standing outside.

The bell above the door tinkled as Grace entered, her refined gait a stark contrast to the hustle of the busy marketplace outside.

'What is a woman of such standing doing in a place like this?' Hetty wondered. *'One thing and one thing only. To cause trouble.'*

"Miss Morgan," Grace greeted her with polished courtesy, her voice a melody of social graces. "How quaint to find you here amongst the loaves. One would almost believe you were preparing a feast."

"Miss Pembroke," Hetty replied, holding her basket closer, like a shield. "I am merely procuring what is needed for my household."

"Indeed," Grace said, her lips curling around the word like silk wrapped around a blade. "One must keep up appearances, even if the reality is less palatable."

Hetty felt a flush creep up her neck, but she stood firm. "Appearances can be deceiving, as we both know. It is the substance beneath that truly matters."

"Substance," Grace echoed, feigning contemplation. "Yes, I suppose some must cling to that notion." She selected a scone delicately, her fingers brushing against Hetty's own. "Especially when there is little else to claim."

"Your words are as filled with meaning as they are with subtlety, Miss Pembroke," Hetty countered, meeting Grace's piercing gaze.

"Ah, but meaning is subjective, and subtlety an art," Grace retorted, stepping back with a flourish. "Do be careful, Hetty. Art can be quite deceptive," Grace said, before gathering her skirts and walking away.

It took a couple of minutes for Hetty's heart to return to its normal rhythm. She took a deep breath in, paid for her wares, and stepped outside the bakers onto the street.

Hetty was unable to shift Grace Pembroke from her mind, whose message was clear. The woman would not yield easily, and the battle lines had just been drawn. What was Hetty to do? With a father suspected of being part of the resurrectionists and now murder, and her precious heart beating only for George Carter, it appeared that Hetty's life was in turmoil. Her father was right, dreams are luxurious for those that can afford them.

Hidden by a copse of elder trees, their leaves whispering secrets to the encroaching dawn, George Carter waited in the sheltered glade just beyond the town's prying eyes. He had to see her, to feel the warmth of her breath on his face, and to feel her words upon his soul in a way that no one had accomplished before.

He looked out from behind the tree and saw the woman who made his heart turn inside out with conflict. "Hetty," he whispered.

Hetty looked around, not expecting to see anybody else on this grim day. Or was it just grim within her questionable mind?

"Hetty," he whispered again, but hopefully loud enough for her to hear.

Hetty stopped and turned around looking for the unsuspecting voice. She saw movement beyond the trees and squinted. Hetty crossed the street and stepped foot into the park. She looked over her shoulder to check she wasn't being followed.

"Dr Carter? Is that you? What are you doing hiding amongst the trees?"

"I had to see you again, Hetty. I have heard the rumours, and I fear it is Grace who is spreading them. I wanted to apologise for her."

"Don't worry yourself, I will be fine."

"But Hetty, she should not be doing that. I fear she is jealous."

"Jealous of what? Of who?"

"Of you."

"Oh?"

"I feel that Lady Pembroke thinks I have feelings for you, and she is jealous of you."

"Why would a lady like that be jealous of me?" For a moment, Hetty imagined herself in George's arms and her hands clasped tightly before her as though they could hold her scattered dreams together.

"Your spirit is bright, and it draws me to you in a way which should be forgiven. But I must marry Grace Pembroke."

"I understand, Dr Carter, I didn't know you harboured such feelings. I suppose being acquainted platonically would be out of the question?"

"Not at all. Grace can't have everything. I feel it's a happy compromise for Grace to marry me but for you to be a platonic friend."

"I'm not sure she would be happy with that proposal."

"Maybe not, but I long for deep conversation with a soul with the same desire as mine."

"Which is?"

"Freedom," he breathed.

The word itself a key to the lock she had placed around her own desires.

"A life where my laughter need not be hushed, and my curiosity can stretch as far as the horizon," he continued.

"Then you must pursue it," she urged gently, admiration lacing her words. "Despite the strictures this world wraps around us." She peered up at him, her piercing eyes lit with the flicker of her resolve. "But there will be a cost. There will be more talk in the town, particularly when I make more enquiries about what is happening. I want to bring an end to the resurrectionists, the murderers, and I want to clear my father's name of all of it."

"Let them talk," he interrupted, a determined edge to his soft tone.

"Easy for you to say, Dr Carter," she teased, a half-smile playing on her lips despite the gravity of their conversation. "You who stand above the gossip and the grime."

"Perhaps," he conceded, a rueful twist to his smile. "But I am bound by expectations no less than chains. And yet here I stand, with a woman who dares to dream of more."

"George, I—" Her voice faltered as she grappled with the weight of her aspirations against the cold reality.

"Hetty," he said, taking a step closer, his presence a solid reassurance amidst her tumultuous thoughts. "Wherever your dreams may lead, my admiration, my affections, they are ..."

"Yes?" she asked, urging him to continue. Her heart skipped with romantic expectation, warmth flooding her chest.

"Nothing. I must not declare my feelings like this when my engagement to Lady Pembroke is due to be announced."

For a moment, Hetty thought Dr Carter was about to voice his true feelings for her. They would have made the grim profession she sought to escape, the soot-stained buildings, and the rigid Victorian etiquette fade into the background, leaving only promise reflected in George's earnest gaze.

"If you are to be with Grace, then there is nothing I can do to stop that."

"I agree, but it doesn't mean I can't help you unravel the truth. I want peace and normality as much as you do in this town. Let me help you, please."

Hetty sighed as she considered the consequences. "I think that would be much appreciated. I will need all the help I can find."

"Good, then we will meet again," George said, with a glint in his eyes that made Hetty believe there may be hope yet for her future with Dr Carter.

From behind a nearby thicket, concealed by shadows and envy, Grace Pembroke watched the pair, her delicate hand tightening around the lace of her parasol. How dare Hetty Morgan meet with George again, she could not and would not allow the undertaker's lass to weave her web of fantasy around George, not when so much depended on her marriage to him. Her grip on the parasol handle intensified, her knuckles turning white.

Chapter Twelve

"Troubled thoughts this evening, George?" The voice of his elder brother, Robert, interrupted his solitary brooding as he entered the room without ceremony.

"Is it that obvious?" George replied, not meeting Robert's gaze.

"Only to one who knows you well." Robert leaned against the doorframe, observing his brother with a discerning eye. "What weighs so heavily on your mind? Is it the engagement?"

"Engagement," George echoed, the word feeling like a leaden weight on his tongue. "Yes, and no. It's Hetty Morgan."

"Ah, the undertaker's lass," Robert said, a note of surprise in his tone. "I would not have expected her name to pass your lips in such a context."

"Nor I," George confessed, striding over to the window where he stared out into the darkness, as if seeking answers in the night. "But my heart refuses to yield to expectations. I find myself drawn to her, Robert. She is unlike any woman I have ever known."

"Drawn to her?" Robert pushed off from the doorframe, concern etching his brow. "I thought you had decided you will marry Grace by duty and familial obligation."

"I did, I will, it's just ..."

"You are falling deeply into Miss Morgan."

George looked up at his brother, his thick, trimmed eyebrows shadowing the conflict in his eyes.

"George, think of the scandal," Robert warned, his voice lowering to an urgent whisper. "Father would never approve, and the Pembrokes wield considerable influence. Not to mention the risks to your own reputation."

"Reputation be damned," George's voice rose in defiance. "Since when did we become slaves to the judgement of society? To hollow titles and empty alliances? Besides, you asked me to think carefully about my marriage to Grace, what has changed your mind?"

"Father has had a word with me. He has heard rumours about you and Miss Morgan. He spoke to me yesterday and asked that I make sure your intentions are still clear with Lady Pembroke."

"Mm, I bet he has."

"What will you do?" Robert asked, a hint of resignation lacing his words.

George sighed, the internal battle waging on. "I do not know. But I cannot ignore the stirrings of my heart, nor can I deny the potential storm that looms on the horizon should I choose to follow it."

"Be careful, brother," Robert advised, stepping closer. "The path of the heart is fraught with peril. You must decide whether love is worth the cost of your family, your reputation, and physician title. I fear that when people hear about you and Miss Morgan, if you decide to break your engagement, you will no longer have patients."

"Indeed," George murmured, uncertainty clouding his thoughtful brown eyes. "And yet if love is to be my downfall, it will be a glorious one."

Chapter Thirteen

Hetty Morgan stood cloaked in the shadow of St. Dunstan's parish church, its spires piercing the fog like accusatory fingers. Her breath fogged before her, each exhalation a whispered ghost of innocence lost. She clutched the locket at her throat—a trinket from her youth, within which was harboured a painted miniature of her mother, smiling with eyes that knew no shadows.

'*Mother believed people were fundamentally good,*' she murmured to the silent graves around her, '*that every soul carried a spark of divine light.*' Hetty closed her eyes, and there, amidst the stone angels and weeping willows, a memory unfolded.

She was seven again, twirling in the meadow behind their old home, her laughter mingling with the rustle of wildflowers. Her father, a man she revered, spun her around until the world blurred into an array of colours, and she truly believed that nothing could ever taint such moments of pure joy.

"Miss Morgan?" The voice, deep and laced with concern, snapped Hetty back to the present. She turned, her heart leaping as George Carter emerged from the mist, his tall form a bastion of steadfastness in these uncertain times.

"Dr Carter," she greeted, her voice betraying none of the tremors that shook her core. "I did not expect you so early."

"Nor did I anticipate finding you among the dead," he replied, his brown eyes searching hers with an intensity that made her feel exposed, vulnerable.

Hetty hesitated, torn between her longing for solace and the fear of revealing too much. "It is my father," she confessed. "I know he is involved in the murders, I just know it."

"Your father is a respected businessman," George assured her, though his gaze did not waver. "These rumours of resurrectionists and murders are unsettling, but—"

"Rumours?" Hetty's voice rose, brittle as the frost underfoot. "But they are more than idle whispers, George. They carry the stench of truth."

"Then we must tread carefully," George said, closing the space between them. "For your sake, and for the peace of this community."

"Peace?" A bitter laugh escaped her, and she quickly pressed a hand to her mouth, as if to capture the sound before it betrayed her further. "There can be no peace when every grave is a bed of suspicion."

"Let us gather what evidence we can," he urged. "Together, we shall navigate these treacherous waters."

THE DAUGHTER'S ENDURING LOVE

"Navigate to what end?" Hetty's blue eyes flashed as she faced him. "To expose my own father? To leave us penniless?"

"No, to clear his name," George countered gently. "You must trust me, Hetty."

"Trust does not fill empty bellies," she retorted.

"Nor does silence protect the innocent," he reminded her softly. "Let us discuss this further."

Nodding, Hetty allowed herself to be led away from the graveyard, her mind a whirlwind of fear and nascent love.

"Come, follow me, I know just the place to visit to find out what people are saying."

Hetty followed tentatively, continuously looking over her shoulder and her heart skipping at a beat at each unsuspecting sound.

As they approached the dimly lit entrance of the local tavern, the heavy wooden door creaked ominously, protesting its constant use. George placed his hand gently but firmly on Hetty's back, urging her forward.

"Are you certain we should be seen here together?" Hetty whispered, her voice barely audible over the raucous laughter spilling from within.

"Appearances be damned," George replied with a steely resolve. "What matters is uncovering the truth."

The warmth of his touch seeped through the fabric of her dress, emboldening her as they stepped into the haze of tobacco smoke and ale that shrouded the tavern's patrons. They found themselves amidst a throng of townsfolk, each one seemingly weighed down by the same cloud of suspicion that had taken residence over the town.

"Mind yourself," George said, leading her to a secluded corner table that offered a clear vantage point of the room. "We're here to listen, not to draw attention."

Hetty nodded, taking a seat across from him. She scanned the room, noting the furrowed brows and downturned mouths. Her heart raced as the snippets of conversation reached her ears, tales of darkness and death weaving through the clinking of glasses.

"Did'ja hear 'bout the latest one? Cold as ice, he was, right in the burial ground," one man slurred to his companion, his eyes wide with morbid fascination.

"Resurrectionists, mark my words," another responded gravely from across the room. "Them devils'll stop at nothin' for a fresh corpse."

A shiver ran down Hetty's spine, and she turned her gaze to George, searching his face for reassurance. "George," she began, her voice quivering slightly, "what if they are right? What if—"

"Shh," he interrupted, placing a finger to his lips. "We mustn't jump to conclusions. Let us gather what we know and present it only when we are certain."

"Certainty is a luxury we may not afford," she countered, her hands clasped tightly beneath the table to still their trembling.

"Then we shall cling to hope," he said, reaching across to cover her hands with his own. His touch was both comforting and electrifying, sending a jolt of courage through her veins.

"Hope," Hetty echoed softly, allowing herself to lean on his strength, if just for a moment.

"Indeed," George affirmed, giving her hands a gentle squeeze before withdrawing. "Now, let us pay heed to the room once more."

Together, they sat in silence, absorbing the words spoken around them, each phrase a piece of the puzzle they were desperate to solve.

"George, look," Hetty's whisper sliced through the din of the tavern as she nudged him with a sense of urgency. Her gaze was locked on a burly man who had risen from his seat, pint in hand, eyes narrowed in their direction.

"Miss Morgan!" the man bellowed, and the room fell into an uneasy hush. "Your father's dealings are tainting this town. It's common knowledge he keeps the company of criminals, the resurrectionists!"

Hetty felt her heart lurch, her breath catching in her throat. George stood swiftly, his chair scraping back against the wooden floor. "Sir, you speak of matters based on hearsay," George stated, his voice even but firm. "Accusations such as these require proof, not idle talk fuelled by ale."

The man sneered, taking a lumbering step closer. "Proof? The dead don't stay buried 'round here, and everyone knows who profits from it."

"Enough!" George's command cut through the whispers that began to swell around them. He turned to Hetty, his brown eyes softening. "Hetty, this is not your burden to bear."

But Hetty felt the weight of her father's sins heavy upon her shoulders. She rose to stand beside George, meeting the man's accusatory glare with a resolve born of desperation. "My father is a man of business," she said, her voice steady despite the tremble in her soul. "He is not a criminal."

"Isn't he now?" the man spat back. "We'll see what the constables have to say about that."

"Let us leave," George murmured close to her ear, ushering her away from the confrontation before it could escalate further.

"Thank you," she said, her voice barely above a whisper as they walked down the cobblestone street, the echo of their steps mingling with the distant clamour of the tavern.

"Hetty," George's voice held a concern that made her insides twist. "You must tell me if there is more to this. Is there anything I should know?"

She looked up at him, his face illuminated by the faint glow of the gas lamps lining the street. Her lips parted, a thousand confessions teetering on the edge of revelation. But fear clutched at her words, turning them into half-truths.

"I fear for my father," she admitted, her blue eyes shimmering with unshed tears. "His associations... they may lead him into trouble. And for you as a physician, will you not get into trouble too for his vile acts if you are associated with me?"

"Come," George said, as they neared another tavern, "let's not tarry here in the open."

Hetty nodded, her heartbeat thrumming in her ears. Together, they slipped through the creaking door of a dimly lit and private establishment, where the stench of ale and tobacco smoke hung heavy. The patrons and interior two classes above those of the last tavern.

They found an unobtrusive corner, their backs to the wall, as Hetty scanned the room with a practised eye.

A huddle of men at the bar spoke in urgent, low tones. One of them, a grizzled fellow with weathered hands, leaned in closer to his companions, whispering something that made the others glance around furtively.

"Can you make out what they're saying?" Hetty whispered to George, trying to keep her voice steady.

"Shh," George cautioned, straining his ears. His hand found hers under the table, a reassuring pressure.

"...unnatural it was," the man's gravelly voice carried faintly to their corner. "The way the body lay, like it had been... prepared for students' knives—"

THE DAUGHTER'S ENDURING LOVE 65

Hetty felt a cold shiver run down her spine. "Prepared?" she echoed under her breath, her mind racing with dreadful images.

"Indeed," George murmured grimly. "It sounds eerily similar to the practices of resurrectionists."

"Which would mean—" Hetty couldn't finish the sentence, the implication too horrifying to voice. Her father's dealings with the anatomy school flashed before her eyes, the late-night visitors, the hushed transactions.

"Let us not jump to conclusions," he continued. "Your father is not the only man in Blackstone who could fall under suspicion."

Hetty and George emerged from the suffocating atmosphere. They had not walked far when the crisp sound of laughter reached their ears. Grace Pembroke stood a few paces away, her blonde hair glinting like spun gold in the last rays of daylight.

"Tell me," Grace said, as she appeared from the shadows. "Are you assisting my future fiancé with some noble cause or embroiling him in affairs he should have nothing to do with as a man of higher class?" Grace looked Hetty up and down as she spoke.

Hetty's cheeks flushed with indignation, but she swallowed the retort that threatened to spill forth. "We were merely discussing matters of importance to Blackstone," she responded evenly.

"Of course," Grace said, her gaze sharp as she turned to George. "One must admire your dedication, Dr Carter. Taking such... personal interest in the town's affairs with a woman with no suitor."

"Miss Pembroke, your concern is noted," George said, his voice firm. "Now, if you'll excuse us."

Hetty could feel Grace's eyes boring into her back, full of misgivings and silent accusations.

"Pay her no mind," George murmured, his arm brushing against hers in a comforting gesture.

"Her words are like barbs," Hetty confessed, blinking back the sting of unshed tears. "She sees only what she wishes to believe."

"Then we shall prove her wrong," he vowed, his hand finding hers and squeezing gently.

"George, I fear what may come of all this," she whispered as they approached her doorstep.

"Whatever dangers lie ahead, I will face them with you," he assured her, his eyes searching hers.

"I do not wish to draw you into my family's troubles," she said, her voice trembling. Her heart swelled with a mixture of love and dread. Could she truly allow George to risk everything for her—a woman whose life was mired in scandal and suspicion?

"Please be careful," she implored, reluctant to release his hand.

"Always," he promised, and with a final glance filled with unsaid promises, he departed into the night.

Alone, Hetty entered her home, the weight of the evening's revelations pressing heavily upon her. The once-familiar surroundings now seemed alien.

In the quiet solitude of her room, Hetty sat by the window, gazing out at the inky sky. Stars twinkled distantly, indifferent to the turmoil below. She clasped her hands together, seeking strength in prayer or perhaps just a moment of peace amidst the storm raging within her.

'Father, what have you done?' she murmured into the silence, a single tear trailing down her cheek.

Hetty walked over to the old mahogany desk that belonged to her father. She pulled open one of the small drawers with a slight frustration. *'Father keeps everything locked away,'* she whispered to herself.

Her hand brushed against a small keyhole hidden beneath a stack of ledgers and a surge of adrenaline prompted her to look around before she remembered the solitude of the hour. She found the key in her father's snuff box and inserted it into the lock.

The click of the mechanism was almost deafening in the hush of the room. She opened the compartment, revealing a stack of papers. Her eye caught sight of a letter, its seal broken, the handwriting unfamiliar and hurried.

'*Dearest Thomas,*' she read aloud, her voice barely above a murmur, '*the merchandise arrived intact, and payment has been rendered unto your account. We do however need more bodies, please can you make the necessary arrangements and further payment will be made ...*'

'Merchandise? More bodies?' Hetty's mind raced. She scanned further down, her eyes widening at each sentence, each word a nail in the coffin of her denial.

Hetty read on. '*Ensure the physician remains unaware of our procurement methods. Your discretion in these matters is, as always, invaluable.*'

'Procurement methods?' Hetty repeated. Her voice cracked, her hands shaking so much that the letter almost slipped from her grasp.

Chapter Fourteen

Hetty Morgan leaned against a cool, brick wall in an alleyway, hidden from the prying eyes of the main thoroughfare. Her blue eyes, usually pools of contemplation and sorrow, now flickered with urgency as she read the hastily scrawled words from Beatrice Pritchard.

"Meet me at dusk," the letter implored, "Chiswick Chapel's steps. Come alone."

Hetty tucked the letter into her coat, her auburn hair momentarily escaping its practical tie to dance in the breeze. She made her way through the maze of cobbled lanes, each step taking her closer to the

THE DAUGHTER'S ENDURING LOVE

heart of the district's unrest—the body-snatching that plagued their community, robbing even the dead of peace.

"Miss Morgan, I feared you wouldn't come," Beatrice said softly as Hetty ascended the chapel steps just as the last light of day succumbed to evening shadows.

"Mrs Pritchard, I could hardly ignore your plea. Your letter was intriguing to say the least. I'm curious." Hetty's voice betrayed a hint of the turmoil within—fear mingled with determination.

"Please, call me Beatrice," Mrs Pritchard insisted, her eyes glinting under the oil lamps. "We haven't much time, and the walls, they have ears," she said, as her eyes looked left and right to check she had not been followed.

"Of course."

They stepped through the door of the church and settled into a secluded pew at the side of the building. "I've heard about your plight, Hetty. The whispers travel fast in the town, especially when one is fighting against the tide."

Hetty clasped her hands tightly in her lap. "I sense you have braved this path before. You wouldn't have gotten in touch with me if you hadn't had experience of the resurrectionists," she murmured, seeking confirmation in the other woman's eyes.

"Indeed, I have," Beatrice acknowledged, a note of bitterness threading her otherwise warm tone. "My attempts were futile then, but together, perhaps we stand a chance. And they took the life of someone I loved dearly." Beatrice looked at her hands and wiped a teardrop that fell onto her cheek.

"Murders most foul, they are," Hetty said, her voice growing steady as she drew strength from Beatrice's presence. Especially when they affect the ones we love. And the implications—, well, they are deeper than I could possibly imagine. Especially if my father is involved."

Beatrice looked at the young woman with compassion. "It's more than just the desecration of graves. We're speaking of the very fabric of society being torn apart and changed for good if somebody doesn't do something."

"I agree. But there is more. We are not just dealing with a few rogue grave robbers here, this is organised, methodical, and profitable for all those involved."

"How do you know? Have you found something?"

"There are entries in ledgers that don't make sense and have amounts paid next to them for unscrupulous reasons. Respected members of society, judges, doctors, the wealthy few … they are named in my father's ledgers."

Beatrice blinked slowly and her eyebrows furrowed together. "Oh, my poor, poor dear. Perhaps there's an explanation, something we're missing."

"Doubtful. And the only thing that breaks my heart in all of this apart from compassion for the families left behind, is my father seems to be involved somehow."

Beatrice sighed. "Let us help you, Hetty. You can't do this alone. We will stand united, gather what we need, help bring the guilty to justice and hope that will stop these torrid murders."

"Can we hope to make a difference?" Hetty asked, the weight of her family's shadow looming over her thoughts.

"Yes we can. We need hope to support what we are doing," Beatrice replied, reaching across to place a comforting hand upon Hetty's. "But with it, we shall wield the truth whatever it takes."

"Your courage gives me heart," Hetty confessed, allowing herself a moment of vulnerability in the safety of their shared conviction. "How did you gather evidence against them before?"

"Carefully," Beatrice said, her lips curving into a wry smile despite the gravity of the conversation. "One must tread lightly around those who would kill for profit. But there are always cracks, even in the well-fortified walls of corruption."

"Then we shall find them," Hetty declared, her resolve hardening like steel. "And bring an end to this blight upon the town."

"Indeed, we shall," Beatrice affirmed. They stood up from their pews and walked down the aisle towards the large wooden doors.

"Frederick!" Beatrice exclaimed. She looked at the imposing figure who had walked through the door. She walked towards her son and gave him an affectionate embrace. "What brings you here at this hour? How did you know I was here?"

"Ma," Frederick said, releasing Beatrice and offering Hetty a courteous nod. "I knew you were meeting Miss Morgan, and I couldn't stay away. The tales of your tenacity, Miss Morgan, have reached even my ears."

Hetty felt her cheeks warm at his words and gave a shy smile. "Mr Pritchard, I am merely trying to do what is right. The priority for me is to clear my father's name, but I don't think that is possible."

"We are here to help," he replied. "We wanted justice for my father but we were warned away. It is your determination that convinces me you are the ally we need. If you'll permit me, I would like to join you in seeking justice for these horrid crimes."

"Your assistance is most welcome, Mr Pritchard," Hetty said, her voice steady despite the flutter in her chest. "But why the sudden interest in the plight?"

"Because," Frederick's expression sobered, "like I said, the resurrectionists took my pa from us. They have torn a chasm through our family, and I seek retribution, as well as peace."

Beatrice's hand found its way to Frederick's shoulder, a silent show of shared grief and resolve.

"I heard. And together, we shall find the evidence to bring them down," Hetty declared, feeling a kinship with these two souls united by loss.

"Quite right, Miss Morgan," Frederick agreed, leaning forward. "We will be thorough and cautious, and through our combined efforts, we'll unravel their ways."

"Your faith gives me hope," Hetty confessed, finding comfort in the solidarity of their shared mission.

The hushed tones of their conspiracy were abruptly interrupted by a sharp knock at the door, causing the trio to exchange anxious glances. Hetty's heart raced; surely, they had been discreet in arranging this meeting?

"Stay here," Beatrice whispered as she walked to the door and turned the handle. She peered around the door when it was suddenly pushed aside, almost knocking Beatrice off her feet.

Hetty held her breath, watching Beatrice's back stiffen. "Miss Pembroke, what an unexpected surprise."

"Beatrice, darling," came a saccharine voice that dripped with false warmth. Grace Pembroke stepped into view, her eyes scanned the room and rested on Hetty. "I was just passing by and couldn't help but notice the light. A late-night gathering, how intriguing."

"Merely discussing some charity work," Beatrice replied smoothly, blocking the doorway with her frame.

"Charity, is it?" Grace's gaze lingered pointedly on Frederick, then flicked back to Hetty. "And Miss Morgan is involved? How... philanthropic of her considering her background. I wouldn't have thought she would have a charitable cell in her body."

"We were about to conclude our affairs, Miss Pembroke, so if you will excuse us."

"Of course, I wouldn't dream of interrupting further." Grace's smile was tight-lipped. "But do be careful, dear Beatrice. These are perilous times, and one never knows who might be entangled in unsavoury business."

Hetty felt the veiled threat in Grace's words, a chill creeping up her spine. The implied accusation hung in the air, tainting the newly formed bond with suspicion.

"Your concern is noted," Beatrice replied, her politeness unyielding. "However, I can make my own decisions when it comes to who I spend my time with."

With a curt nod, Grace turned on her heel. The rustle of her skirts echoing down the chapel aisle as she left.

Beatrice let out a long sigh.

"Grace Pembroke has always been skilled at weaving her own narratives," Hetty said quietly. Her hands gripped the back of a pew, her knuckles turning white.

"We must be cautious," Frederick added, his youthful face set with determination. "We cannot afford to be undermined by the likes of her."

"Indeed," Beatrice agreed. "Which is why you must stay with us, Hetty. Our home is your sanctuary."

Hetty hesitated, the offer a beacon of safety amidst the swirling doubts and fears. "But Beatrice, I can't. I don't want my father to either suspect what I am doing, or to be left on his own."

"But it will be safer with us," Beatrice interjected firmly.

"Thank you, your generosity knows no bounds. But I must stay with him."

"Very well, we understand, don't we, Ma? We will just have to be discreet and careful when we meet."

"And we must find proof before we cast stones, even in our minds."

"Proof..." she echoed, the word lingering between them like a lifeline.

"Let us devise a plan," Frederick suggested. "We'll scour every corner of the town for evidence. We have to start somewhere."

"Where?" Hetty asked, the weight of the task settling upon her shoulders.

"Perhaps the anatomy school," he mused. "Follow the trail of bodies sold, see where it leads."

Hetty nodded slowly, determination knitting her brows. "But how do we proceed without arousing suspicion?" What if we encounter resistance?" Hetty inquired, her mind racing with possibilities.

"Then we keep going as best we can until we have what we need."

"Very well," Hetty agreed, allowing herself a small smile.

Chapter Fifteen

⁓⋆⋅✦⋅⋆⁓

The narrow confines of the Blackstone constabulary office were thick with the scent of oil and leather. Constable Wells, a stocky man with a bristling moustache, shuffled through a stack of papers on his desk.

Hetty stood opposite him, her hands clenched in the folds of her skirt to steady her nerves. She had been called to attend the office and collect something of value.

"Miss Morgan," Constable Wells began, clearing his throat. "This here was found near the body." With a grave face, he slid a small, velvet pouch across the desk towards her.

Hetty's breath hitched as she drew out a signet ring from the pouch, the crest unmistakably that of her family's undertaking business. Her father's ring. The metal felt cold against her trembling fingertips, but it burned like a brand, searing her with implications too distressing to voice.

"Why are you telling me?"

"Because, Miss, I have tried to call on your father but there is never any response."

"I apologise, he has a lot of work to do at the moment. We need the money desperately, and my father has a reputation to uphold."

"Indeed he has, being the main undertaker in the town."

"And you are certain this was at the scene?" Her voice was barely a whisper, laced with dread.

"Quite certain, Miss." The constable's eyes held a measure of sympathy, yet they did not stray from their professional resolve.

"Thank you, Constable." Hetty tucked the ring back into the pouch, her mind a swirl of confusion and fear. How had her father's ring ended up there? Could it be mere coincidence?

"Miss Morgan," Constable Wells hesitated, "I understand this is difficult, but we need to—"

"Difficult?" Hetty cut in, her composure threatening to crack. "It is far more than that. This could implicate my father in horrors unspeakable."

"Which is why we must ask—"

"Excuse me, Constable," George Carter interjected, striding into the room with a purposeful air that demanded attention. His gaze fixed on Hetty with deep concern. "Is everything quite alright?"

"George?" The sight of Dr Carter took her breath away yet again. "What are you doing here? This is not a coincidence, is it?" Hetty frowned a little, not knowing who to trust.

"It is merely a coincidence, Hetty. I was here on some business I had to consult the constabulary with and heard your voice."

"Dr Carter," Constable Wells acknowledged with a curt nod, "this is a private matter."

"Whatever affects Miss Morgan concerns me as well," said George firmly, offering Hetty a supportive glance.

"Your concern is noted, but I'm afraid this is no business of yours."

"I agree!" came a stern voice from the doorway. William, George's father, loomed over the scene, his blue eyes sharp and unwavering. "Come with me, George, we must leave."

"No, Father, I must help Miss Morgan."

"George, your interference in such matters is unbecoming of our family name," William said, unable to meet Hetty's eyes.

"Father, I cannot simply stand by when a friend is in distress," George protested, his stance resolute.

"Friendship is one thing; sullying the Carter reputation is quite another." William's tone was icy, carrying an implicit threat.

"Reputation," George scoffed, "What value is there in a reputation if it stands upon indifference to injustice?"

"George!" Hetty exclaimed, her heart pounding. "Please, do not argue on my account. Go with your father."

"Miss Morgan deserves our support, not our silence," George replied, his eyes meeting hers with unwavering conviction.

"Enough," William snapped, turning to leave. "We shall discuss this at home, and you will remember your place, George."

"Of course, Father," George said, though his jaw was set in quiet defiance.

"Miss Morgan," Constable Wells interjected once more, "the investigation must proceed. Will you cooperate?"

Hetty drew herself up, clutching the velvet pouch like a lifeline. "Yes, Constable. I will do whatever is necessary to clear my father's name."

"Very well, not that I believe your father isn't guilty. However, he has done good in the town over many years, seeing to the dead, laying them to rest, giving them befitting burials. But I must warn you, if he is found to be involved in these torrid crimes, then he must be punished. We shall keep you informed."

Hetty nodded briefly before slipping the pouch into her pocket and leaving the constabulary office. Her pulse quickened as she stepped into the bustling market square. The scent of fresh bread from nearby stalls made her feel hungry. She hadn't eaten in hours, the thought of food being pushed to the back of her mind, her father's dealings taking priority.

"Miss Morgan," Grace called out, her voice carrying effortlessly over the din, "how fortuitous to find you here amongst the common folk."

Hetty clenched her fists, steadying her breath. "Miss Pembroke," she replied evenly, "to what do I owe this encounter? Anyone would think you are following me around. I didn't know you existed a week ago, now it seems you can't leave my side. Surely you must have other business to address?"

"I am merely concerned for the well-being of our community," Grace said, her lips curling into a facade of concern. "It is distressing, is it not, that we find ourselves amidst such ghastly business? Bodysnatching and murder."

"It is a matter of great concern," Hetty conceded, aware of the growing circle of onlookers. She could feel their eyes upon her, their whispers weaving a web of suspicion.

Grace held up a delicate handkerchief, theatrically dabbing at her eyes. "And to think, dear Hetty, that your own father might be entangled in these sordid deaths." Her voice rose dramatically. "Why, the very ring he wears was found at the scene of a crime!"

The murmurings of the crowd swelled into a cacophony of gasps and tuts. Hetty felt a cold dread settle in her stomach, but she lifted her chin defiantly.

"Accusations without proof are as flimsy as your concern, Miss Pembroke," Hetty shot back. "My father is an honourable man."

"Is he?" Grace arched an eyebrow, her green eyes glinting with malice. "Or is he merely skilled at deception, much like his daughter?"

Before Hetty could muster a reply, a reassuring presence appeared at her side—Beatrice Pritchard, her expression a blend of fierce loyalty and indignation.

"Your insinuations are unwarranted, Miss Pembroke," Beatrice interjected, her tone unwavering. "Hetty has been working tirelessly to prove her father's innocence and finding the guilty party. Hetty wants peace and justice for this town as much as anybody else."

"Does she now?" Grace's gaze flickered between the two women, assessing the solidarity before her.

"Indeed," Hetty affirmed, bolstered by Beatrice's support. "And I will not be deterred by baseless gossip or your attempts at intimidation."

"Intimidation?" Grace feigned shock, placing a gloved hand over her heart. "I am merely expressing the concerns that many share."

"That may be so, Miss Pemberton, but I also believe you are fabricating your concerns because of me. If your fiancé wasn't a good friend of mine, I'm sure you would leave the gossip alone. Instead, you feel threatened by my presence," Hetty tried not to allow her bottom lip to tremble with emotion.

"Hetty is right. Perhaps you should focus on helping find the true culprits rather than casting unwarranted aspersions," Beatrice retorted, standing shoulder to shoulder with Hetty.

The crowd murmured, some nodding in agreement with Beatrice's sentiment. Hetty sensed the tide of public opinion wavering, uncertain.

"Very well," Grace said, her composure slipping ever so slightly. "Let the truth come to light, as it surely will." With a final, scathing look, she turned on her heel and departed, the rustle of her skirts a whisper of menace.

As the tension in the air dissipated, Hetty felt a profound gratitude for Beatrice's intervention. "Thank you," she breathed, feeling the weight of isolation lift ever so slightly. Her head felt light, and it took all of her strength not to faint.

"Think nothing of it," Beatrice replied with a warm smile and grasped her friend's arm lightly. "We women must stand together, especially in times such as these."

The crowd slowly dispersed after Grace's departure, leaving a heavy silence in its wake. Hetty's heart still raced, but Beatrice's arm around her shoulders was a steadying force.

"Let us retire to my home," Beatrice suggested with a gentle tug. "We can speak more freely there."

"I could use a moment of respite," Hetty admitted, allowing herself to be led away from the scene that had just unfolded.

They walked the slippery cobblestone streets. The echoes of their footsteps mingling with the distant sounds of costermongers, the call of street vendors, clatter of horse-drawn carriages, and the ever-present murmur of the Thames in the background.

Chapter Sixteen

Beatrice's front door closed behind them with a reassuring thud, shutting out the world and its prying eyes. Beatrice led Hetty into the front room.

The fire was lit and Hetty noticed the room was comfortably furnished, although modest. Frederick was sat in an armchair, his face aglow from the fire.

"Hetty, are you unharmed?" Frederick asked, rising from his seat promptly when he saw the two women enter.

"More shaken than hurt, but yes, I am unharmed, thank you," Hetty replied, taking a seat.

"Grace Pembroke has crossed a line," Beatrice said, her voice firm as she poured tea for both of them. "But we will not let her falsehoods sway us."

"Indeed," Frederick added, handing a cup to Hetty. "It only strengthens our mission." Frederick crossed the room to a small table in the corner. He picked up a sealed letter. "This arrived for you, Hetty," he said, passing the note to her.

"Who could it be from?" Beatrice asked, peering over curiously. "Especially as it has been delivered here instead of your own home, how strange."

Hetty turned the note over in her hands; it bore no seal or marking. Her fingers trembled slightly as she broke the wax-less fold. She scanned the contents quickly, her blue eyes widening with each word.

"Hetty? What is it?" Frederick leaned forward; his youthful face lined with anxiety.

"It's a warning," Hetty whispered, her voice barely above a hush. "From someone who claims to know the resurrectionists' next move."

"Read it aloud," Beatrice urged, moving closer.

"*Miss Morgan,*" Hetty began, her voice steady despite the trembling of the paper.

'Your inquiries have not gone unnoticed. Cease your meddling or suffer the consequences. The dead are not the only ones who can be silenced.'

A chill swept through the room, and the trio exchanged a series of grave looks. "It seems we've rattled some cages," Frederick said after a beat, his jaw set.

"But how did they know?" Hetty enquired.

"Know what?"

"Where I would be, Frederick. They must have followed us back here. Why would they deliver the letter here?"

"They may be desperate," Frederick finished for her. "They probably didn't want your father to know they are on to you."

"Desperation leads to recklessness," Beatrice pointed out. "And that can work in our favour. We must remain vigilant and stand united."

"Agreed," Hetty nodded, a newfound determination lighting her gaze. "I refuse to be intimidated by shadows and gossip mongers."

"Then let us plan our next steps," Frederick suggested, "and bring an end to this macabre trade, once and for all."

"Tomorrow," Hetty said firmly, tucking the ominous note into the folds of her dress. "Tonight, we rest and gather our strength."

"Very well," Beatrice conceded, her eyes held the same unyielding spark as Hetty's.

"Tomorrow," Frederick echoed, a silent vow hanging between them.

Chapter Seventeen

Grace Pembroke stood before the ornate mirror in her bedchamber, her reflection a pale ghost in the fading afternoon light. The woman who gazed back at her was a stranger – gone was the confident, assured socialite, replaced by a figure haunted by secrets and doubt.

Her fingers traced the intricate embroidery of her gown, a gown she had ordered for her engagement party. Now, it hung in her wardrobe, a mocking reminder of dreams unravelled and futures uncertain.

A soft knock at the door startled her from her reverie. "Come in," she called, straightening her posture and schooling her features into a mask of composure.

Her mother, entered, her face tight with barely concealed anxiety. "Grace, darling, your father wishes to speak with you. He's in his study."

Grace nodded, a tendril of fear curling in her stomach. These summons to her father's study had become more frequent of late, each one leaving her feeling more trapped, more complicit in affairs she scarcely understood.

As she made her way through the hushed corridors of Pembroke Manor, Grace's mind raced. How had it come to this? When had the clear path of her future – marriage to George, a life of privilege and influence – become so tangled, so fraught with danger?

She paused outside her father's study, taking a deep breath to steel herself before knocking.

"Enter," came the curt response.

Lord Pembroke sat behind his massive oak desk, his face grave as he regarded his daughter. "Grace, sit down. We have much to discuss."

As Grace lowered herself into the chair across from her father, she couldn't help but notice the strain around his eyes, the slight tremor in his usually steady hands.

"You've heard the rumours, I presume?" Lord Pembroke began without preamble. "The whispers about our family, about our associates?"

Grace nodded, her throat too tight for words.

"They must be stopped," her father continued, his voice hard. "The Morgan girl and her meddling friends are becoming a nuisance. They're digging too deep, asking questions that cannot be answered."

"Father," Grace began hesitantly, "perhaps if we were to come forward, to explain—"

"Explain?" Lord Pembroke scoffed, his face darkening. "There is nothing to explain, Grace. What we do, we do for the greater good.

For the advancement of science and medicine. The common folk, with their small minds and superstitious fears, could never understand."

Grace felt a chill run down her spine at her father's words. The conviction in his voice, the unwavering belief in the righteousness of their cause, frightened her more than any whispered rumour or veiled threat.

"But, Father," she pressed on, summoning her courage, "the bodies, the families left to mourn at empty graves, surely there must be another way?"

Lord Pembroke's eyes flashed with anger. "There is no other way, Grace. Progress demands sacrifice. History will vindicate us, even if the present condemns us."

He leaned forward, his voice dropping to a harsh whisper. "You must do your part, my dear. Your engagement to George Carter is more crucial now than ever. We need his family's influence, their connections."

Grace felt her heart constrict. "And they need ours. But George is growing distant. I fear he suspects something about this family."

"Then you must redouble your efforts," her father snapped. "Charm him, distract him. Whatever it takes to keep him, and his interfering conscience, in line."

As the full weight of her father's expectations settled upon her, Grace felt something within her begin to crack. The life she had envisioned, the future she had taken for granted, was slipping away, replaced by a web of lies and moral compromise.

"And if I refuse?" The words escaped her lips before she could stop them, hanging in the air between them like a challenge.

Lord Pembroke's face hardened, all pretence of fatherly concern vanishing. "Then you will share in the consequences, Grace. Make no mistake, we are all in this together. The fall of the Pembrokes would simply be unacceptable, we can't even imagine what would happen."

Grace nodded numbly, recognising the threat beneath his words. As she rose to leave, her father's voice stopped her at the door.

"Remember, Grace. Family above all else. We cannot afford weakness or sentiment, not now."

She left the study, her steps echoing hollowly in the empty corridor. The Grace Pembroke who had entered that room – conflicted but still hopeful – was gone. In her place stood a woman on the precipice of a terrible choice.

As she returned to her chambers, Grace caught sight of herself in a passing mirror. The stranger who stared back at her now bore the weight of an impossible decision. Should she cling to the safety of her family's influence, burying her doubts along with the victims of their ambition? Or should she risk everything – her status, her security, perhaps even her life – to do what she knew in her heart was right?

Chapter Eighteen

Hetty Morgan pressed her ear against the cold wood of the parlour door, the grain rough against her cheek. Her father's voice, a low rumble of discontent, filtered through the cracks.

"Damned carelessness is what it is!" Thomas Morgan's words were sharp as flint strikes. "The cadaver was meant to be fresh, not riddled with putrefaction."

"Wasn't our fault," a gruffer voice countered from within the shadowed room, thick with working-class lilt and defensiveness. "Billingsly's the one who bungled it—left the body out too long."

"Silence!" Another voice hissed, its owner unseen. "Keep your voices down unless you want Mr Grayson sniffing about."

Hetty's breath hitched, her hands balling into fists within the folds of her skirt. She knew these men by their voices, these resurrectionists who trafficked in the dead. Their presence filled the house with an invisible miasma that clung to the drapes and seeped into the floorboards.

"Payment has been made, and what we received was not worth half the coin," her father insisted, anger laced with desperation. His silhouette paced back and forth behind the frosted glass window of the door.

"Be that as it may," a figure replied, cloaked more in darkness than cloth, "we take risks to procure what you sell. Payment is payment, Mr Morgan."

'*Risks?*' Hetty murmured to herself, her heart thrumming like a caged bird against her ribs. How many times had she lain awake at night, listening to the tell-tale signs of her father's nocturnal dealings?

"Then consider this a final warning," her father declared, the underlying threat making Hetty shiver despite the warmth of the hearth nearby. "I will not pay for incompetence, nor will I be swindled by the likes of you."

"Nor will we be cheated by an undertaker playing a gentleman," retorted the gruff voice.

"Enough, enough," came a placating murmur from another figure. "Let's not part on ill terms. We all have much to lose, Mr Morgan."

Hetty's stomach twisted into knots. The resurrectionists spoke true; their dark business was a precarious balance of greed and necessity. She pulled away from the door, her mind racing. Could there be an end to this perpetual night? A way to step into the light without the weight of unspoken crimes?

As the door creaked open, the men filed out, faces obscured by hats pulled low. They spared her no glance, treating her as nothing more than another piece of furniture. Hetty watched them go, their shadows merging with the cobblestone street beyond the flickering gaslight.

"Father," she began, stepping into the parlour only after the last footfall faded into the evening mist. "Must we continue this trade?"

Thomas Morgan's eyes met hers, those deep wells of sorrow and resolve reflecting the dim glow of the oil lamp. "It's our survival, Hetty. Without it, we're naught but paupers waiting for the parish's mercy."

"But at what cost?" Her voice wavered, anxiety knotting her throat as tightly as the corset cinched around her waist.

"Survival always comes at a cost, my child." He turned away from her, his shoulders heavy as if bearing the weight of Blackstone itself. "You must understand, I do this for us—"

"Your time is up, Morgan!" bellowed a rough voice from beyond the threshold.

Thomas Morgan, his face flushed with fury and veins bulging at his temples, walked to the entrance and saw a group of men outside. Hawkins and his fellow resurrectionists hadn't left.

Hetty ran to the back of the parlour on her father's instruction. She hid behind the door and pulled her hand to her mouth, biting the wicks of her fingernails.

"Your threats mean naught to me, Hawkins," Thomas spat out, his stance rigid against the encroaching darkness. "You'll not see another penny until the quality of your merchandise improves."

"Quality?" The leader of the shadowy figures stepped forward, the menace in his voice sharp as a scalpel. "We provide what you ask for, and you'll pay for it, one way or another."

Hetty's hands clenched into fists at her sides, her knuckles whitening. She felt a chill snake its way down her spine as she recalled the whispers that haunted Blackstone's fog-drenched alleys—stories of graves desecrated, and the dead snatched from their eternal slumber. The resurrectionists were ruthless, their business a macabre dance with the devil, supplying the anatomy schools that hungered for cadavers to dissect and study. And they were threatening her father.

"Enough!" Thomas's voice cracked like a whip. "I will not be cowed by your kind. I have friends in high places; do not think I stand alone."

"Friends?" sneered Hawkins. "We both know your kind of friends, Morgan. How long before they turn their backs on you?"

As the tension mounted, Hetty edged closer, her gaze locked on her father's agitated profile. Memories surfaced unbidden: late-night dealings shrouded in secrecy, the muffled thud of heavy sacks, and the metallic scent of blood intermingled with earth. This was the grim reality that underpinned their existence—the lifeblood of their funeral parlour. It had gotten worse since her father was involved with the murders, she was convinced of it.

"Father," Hetty said, her voice steady despite the tremors within, "please, tell them to go!"

"Stay out of this, Hetty," Thomas warned without turning, the threat in his tone directed at the men before him. "You lot, get out! We'll settle our accounts in due course."

The resurrectionist named Hawkins squinted towards the back of the parlour at Hetty, his gaze lingering with a hint of recognition before he grudgingly signalled to his companions. They shuffled out, the promise of retribution hanging heavy in the air.

"Father," Hetty pressed once they were alone, her eyes beseeching, "this must end. We cannot continue to live under such a pall."

"Live?" Thomas exhaled wearily, his anger dissipating into resignation. "We barely survive, child. And survival comes at a cost I'm willing to pay for your sake."

"Even if it damns us both?" Her voice was a whisper, but it cut through the disquieting stillness with the precision of a surgeon's blade.

"Damnation has long been the companion of progress, Hetty." Thomas's gaze met hers. "It is the currency of our age, and we are all indebted to its call," Thomas said, storming off towards the back of the parlour.

The tinkling bell above the shop door heralded a new presence, slicing through the tension. Hetty glanced up, her heart skipping in anticipation and not solely from fear. George Carter stood just inside the threshold, a crate of linens in his arms—a guise for the concern etched deep within his brown eyes.

"Miss Morgan," he greeted with a nod, setting the supplies down with a gentle thud. "I trust I find you well today?"

"Dr Carter," Hetty responded, managing a small smile. "Yes, thank you. I am as well as can be expected. But what brings you here? Why the linens?"

"I used it as an excuse to see you Hetty," he whispered. "I had to see you and it appears I have arrived at the right time. You know you can confide in me if there is anything amiss."

Hetty's gaze flitted about the room, ensuring they were alone. Her father had retreated to the back, likely to brood over ledgers and debts.

"Thank you, Dr Carter," she replied, her fingers twisting at the fabric of her skirt. "Your concern is most comforting."

He studied her carefully, his expression softening. "Your eyes betray a storm, Miss Morgan. One far graver than mere business worries."

THE DAUGHTER'S ENDURING LOVE 93

She felt the weight of truth in his words and the burden of her loyalty. Her father's dealings cast long shadows, and now those shadows threatened to engulf the one glimmer of light in her life—George.

"Business is our livelihood, yet it burdens my conscience," she confessed, her voice barely above a hushed tone. "I fear the path we tread may lead to ruin, both of spirit and flesh."

"Hetty," he said, daring to use her given name with tender insistence. "Your spirit is the last vestige of purity in this mire. It mustn't be tarnished by the misdeeds of others, even those bound by blood."

"Yet how can I detach myself when my own survival is tethered to his choices?" She met his gaze squarely, her eyes searching for his. "How can I dream of a future that may never come to pass because of a past I cannot escape?"

"Because, Miss Morgan," George reached out, pausing just shy of touching her hand, an unspoken promise hanging between them, "we are more than the sum of our lineage, more than the deeds done in desperation. There is a horizon beyond this town, one where honour and love preside."

"Love?" The word escaped her lips before she could rein it in, her heart fluttering against its cage.

"Indeed," George affirmed, his voice steadfast. "A force mightier than any darkness we face."

Hetty felt torn asunder, her loyalty to her father warring with the burgeoning affection for the man before her. Yet in George's earnest gaze, she saw the reflection of a noble soul, one who might just hold the key to unlocking the chains her heritage had wrought.

"Perhaps," she whispered, allowing herself the faintest sprig of hope. "Perhaps love does indeed hold such power."

A heavy silence fell upon the room as the last of George's earnest words lingered in the air.

Chapter Nineteen

The rickety sign of Morgan's funeral parlour creaked as a young street seller pushed open the door. "Here you are, Miss," he said, tilting his cap slightly and throwing the parcel wrapped in brown paper and twine onto the desk where Hetty was standing.

"Excuse me, excuse—"

Hetty's words were fruitless. The young boy had left as quick as he had arrived and outstayed his welcome.

Hetty hastily opened the parcel and unravelled a pile of notes. Her eyes widened as she picked up the pile of money and fingered the thin pieces of paper. *'My, there must be at least ...'*

A handwritten note had settled in the brown paper. She placed the money on the desk and opened the letter.

'*Take this with my love and kindness and give it to your father, he must pay off those wretched men, so you stay safe.*'

Hetty gasped. She did not need to guess who the note was from. '*He must have heard the commotion before he came in yesterday,*' she pondered.

She picked up the pile of notes, put them in one of her pockets along with the letter, and threw the brown paper and twine in the bin.

The door above the bell rang out and she looked up quickly, her cheeks turned pink as if she had been caught doing wrong.

Her brief moment of solace was shattered as Mr William Carter's imposing form loomed at the door. "I'm glad I have you on your own."

"Hello, Mr Carter, what can I do for you?"

"You can stay away from my son. I want you to have nothing more to do with him. He is marrying Grace and that's the end of it. Stay away I tell you, or you will attract more trouble than you are already dealing with. Here, take this as a gift, then don't contact my son again."

Hetty looked down at the pile of notes that Mr Jennings shifted towards her. '*People are throwing money at me today,*' she mused. Hetty picked up the pile of money, enough to pay off the resurrectionists, clear her father's name, and live a frugal yet fruitful life with no concerns. She bit her bottom lip and considered accepting the payment.

The bell above the door rang out once more.

Hetty looked up and a glint returned to her eyes, a smile broadening across her young features. "Dr Carter!" she cried.

"Father," George acknowledged, his tone guarded. "What are you doing here?"

In a moment's decision, Hetty knew what she was about to do would either be the biggest mistake she had ever made, or the act that would secure her future with the man she loved.

"He came to give me this," Hetty said, her hand shaking and holding up the pile of notes.

William's cheeks turned bright red, a flush that travelled down his neck and beyond beneath his shirt.

"Your father gave me this to make me stay away."

George looked at Hetty, doubting her for just a moment that maybe she would choose to take it over his love.

"But I said no," Hetty said, sliding the money along the desk back towards Mr Carter.

George relaxed a little; Hetty had proved her love for him. "Is that right, Father? You came here to pay Hetty to stay away?"

"Well—well—I—erm, it wasn't quite like that, no."

"So, what was it like, Mr Carter? I would not lie."

"George." William Carter's voice was like gravel. "A word, if you please."

"Of course." George stepped forward, his posture rigid.

Hetty watched, a silent observer to the confrontation as father faced son in the pale moonlight.

"Your dalliance with the undertaker's daughter," William began, each word laced with contempt, "it ends now."

"Hetty is—"

"Below us. And your continued association with her threatens more than just your reputation—it jeopardises our family's standing and, consequently, our business interests."

"I will not be swayed from what is right," George replied.

"Very well." William's eyes turned cold, the finality in his voice sending a chill through Hetty's bones. "You've made your choice."

With that, he stalked off, leaving silence and the heavy scent of impending change in his wake.

Chapter Twenty

※

"Hetty?" Her father's voice, unexpected and close, jolted her from her thoughts. "I thought you would be in bed!"

She opened her eyes to find Thomas Morgan standing in the doorway looking bedraggled, his figure cast in the dim light that spilled from the hallway. His gaunt face appeared more drawn than usual, his eyes darting around the room as if searching for unseen threats.

"Father! I wanted to wait up for you, I was concerned for you. I thought you were—"

"Never mind what you thought," he interrupted, his voice a low growl. "Go to bed. It's late."

"But Father, you look—"

"Go!"

She hesitated, biting back the concern that knotted her throat, then gave a small nod, retreating toward her chamber. She paused at the threshold, glancing back to see him slump into an armchair, his head in his hands.

"Is everything all right?" she ventured, despite the warning edge in his tone.

"Everything is fine," he said, though his voice betrayed him, quivering with barely concealed fear. "Just mind your own affairs, Hetty."

"Father, if we are in danger—"

"Enough!" He slammed a fist against the armrest, causing her to flinch. "Do as I say!"

With her heart pounding against her ribcage, Hetty retreated to her room but did not go to bed. Instead, she sat by the window, peering out into the darkness where the confrontation had occurred. Her gaze lingered on the empty street, the chill of dread seeping into her bones.

'*Geroge,*' she whispered into the silence, her breath misting the glass. '*What are we to do?*'

But there was no answer, only the distant echo of her own fears and the heavy sense of foreboding that now hung over the house.

There came a harsh rap of a fist against the parlour door.

"Thomas!" a gruff voice barked from outside. "We need words!"

Hetty put her ear to the door, willing herself not to cry at her father's reaction when he had come home from the tavern smelling of liquor.

"Keep your voice down, you fool," Thomas hissed as he unbolted the door. Shadows spilled into the room as three men cloaked in dark garb shuffled in. The tallest, a gaunt figure with hollow cheeks, stepped forward.

"Where's our payment, Morgan? The job went sour because of your shoddy directions," he growled, his eyes gleaming with malice.

"Shoddy? My information was precise," Mr Morgan retorted, standing his ground despite the tremble in his voice.

"Was it now?" the man sneered. "Then explain why we found ourselves intercepted by constables, eh? Nearly got thrown in Newgate for your blunder."

"Enough," Thomas demanded, but his voice wavered. "I'll get your money, just—"

"Time's up, Morgan." The threat was palpable, and Hetty could bear it no longer.

"Please!" Hetty cried as she swung the door open. She stepped forward, her voice steady though her hands shook. "My father is an honourable man. He will make this right."

"Stay out of this, girl," the gaunt man snapped, but his companions' gazes lingered on her with unsettling interest.

"Indeed, Hetty, return to your room," her father ordered, but there was a plea hidden beneath the command.

She hesitated, torn between obedience and the urge to defend. "No! I won't! Here!" she said, taking the pile of notes from her pocket. Take this and go, we don't want to see you again."

The filthy rascals who had been sent to collect payment, and Thomas, didn't know how to react.

Thomas looked from the money to Hetty and back again. "Hetty, where did you—?"

"It doesn't matter. What does matter is that these horrid men leave now and never return."

The tallest of the three men who had scars across his face and one eye missing, fingered through the notes.

"You don't need to count it," Hetty said. It's all there, and then some. Now be away with you."

The scrawny looking, working class resurrectionary shoved the money in his pocket and fled, his accomplices followed.

"Hetty, where did you get that?"

"It's none of your business, Father. Consider the matter closed." Hetty turned around and made her way to bed leaving Thomas standing in the middle of the room, flabbergasted.

A tear came to his eye feeling grateful for his daughter and the temporary relief from being battered and bruised for non-payment. But how long the relief would last, who knew. Because there was still work to be done and there was nothing Thomas could do about that.

Chapter Twenty-One

Hetty's hands trembled as she gripped the crumpled letter, the ink smudged by her tears. The words seemed to blur before her eyes, but their meaning was seared into her mind. Her father's betrayal cut deeper than any knife.

The door creaked open, and Thomas Morgan entered, his shoulders stooped under the weight of his burdens. He paused, taking in the sight of his daughter's anguished face and the damning evidence in her hand.

"Hetty, what troubles you so?" His voice was gentle, but a flicker of apprehension crossed his features as he glanced at the letter.

She looked up, her blue eyes blazing with a mixture of hurt and anger. "How could you, Father? After all I've done, all the sacrifices I've made. I thought we were finished with this wretched business when I paid off those resurrectionists!"

Thomas flinched as if struck. He reached out a placating hand. "Hetty, please, let me explain--"

"Explain what? That you've continued to deal with those vile body snatchers behind my back? That the money I scraped together meant nothing?" Her voice rose with each accusation, echoing off the bare walls.

He shook his head, desperation etched into the lines of his face. "It's not that simple, Hetty. There are forces at work here that you don't understand."

She scoffed, the sound harsh and bitter. "Oh, I understand perfectly well. You've chosen to betray your own daughter, to drag our family deeper into this mire of sin and shame."

Thomas stepped forward, his hand outstretched. "Please, Hetty, if you would only listen—"

But she recoiled from his touch as if burned.

Thomas ran a hand through his greying hair, his eyes darting around the room as if seeking an escape from his daughter's piercing gaze. "I had no choice, Hetty. The orders came from above, from those who hold our very lives in their hands."

She narrowed her eyes, disbelief etched into every line of her face. "Orders? From whom? What power could possibly compel you to commit such atrocities?"

He shook his head, a bitter laugh escaping his lips. "You have no idea the forces at play here, the strings that bind us all. To defy them would be to sign our own death warrants."

Hetty's heart clenched at the despair in her father's voice, but she steeled herself against the flicker of empathy. "And what of the lives you've taken, the families you've destroyed? Do their deaths mean nothing to you?"

Thomas flinched, his eyes glistening with unshed tears. "Of course they do, Hetty. Each one weighs upon my soul like a millstone. But what choice do I have? To refuse would be to condemn us all to ruin."

She shook her head, her voice rising in a crescendo of anger and pain. "No, Father. You had a choice. You could have confided in me, sought my help. Instead, you chose to lie, to betray everything I believed about you."

He reached for her, his hands trembling. "Please, Hetty, try to understand. I did this for us."

But she stepped back, her eyes hardening with resolve. "No. You did this for yourself, to save your own skin at the cost of innocent lives. I can't bear to look at you, to call you my father."

Hetty's voice, though trembling, cut through the heavy silence that hung between them. "I can't do this anymore. I can't carry the weight of your sins upon my soul."

Thomas' eyes widened, a flicker of panic dancing within their depths. He took a step forward, his hands outstretched in a desperate plea. "Hetty, please. You must understand. I had no choice. I did this for us, for our family."

She shook her head, her auburn hair catching the dim light of the parlour. "No! You did this for yourself. You chose to align yourself with those... those monsters, even after I sacrificed everything to make it right."

"Sacrificed?" Thomas scoffed, a bitter laugh escaping his lips. "What do you know of sacrifice, child? I have given everything, my very soul, to keep this family afloat. To keep you safe and provided for."

Hetty's eyes flashed with a newfound strength, a resolve born from the ashes of her shattered illusions. "And what of my safety, Father? What of my soul? You've tainted us both with your actions, your lies. I can't bear it any longer."

Thomas' face crumpled, the weight of his daughter's words striking him like a physical blow. He reached for her, his voice breaking. "Hetty, please. I need you. I need your understanding, your forgiveness."

But Hetty stepped back, her heart hardening against the man she once idolised. "Forgiveness?" she whispered, her voice laced with pain. "How can I forgive what you've done? What you have become?"

A single tear slipped down Thomas' weathered cheek, a silent testament to the depth of his despair. "I'm still your father, Hetty. Doesn't that count for something?"

For a moment, Hetty wavered, the flicker of empathy that had ignited within her threatening to overtake her resolve. But the contents of the letter confirming her father's involvement in the murders, and the stark evidence of her father's betrayal, steeled her heart once more.

"I'm sorry," she said softly, her voice filled with a quiet determination. "But I cannot walk this path with you any longer. I will not let your sins define me, define our family. I must break free, before it's too late."

With those final words, Hetty turned away, her skirts swishing against the worn floorboards as she moved towards the door. Thomas watched her go, his heart shattering with each step, the weight of his choices crushing down upon him like a physical force.

As Hetty's hand grasped the cool metal of the doorknob, she paused, a final thought whispered into the heavy air between them. *'I love you, Father. But I cannot save you from yourself.'*

Hetty stood motionless for a moment, her hand gripping the faded brass handle on the door, her eyes fixed on the worn grains of the wood. She fought to steady her breathing, to quell the tempest of emotions that threatened to overwhelm her. Anger, betrayal, and a profound sense of loss warred within her heart, each vying for dominance.

'I had to do it,' she told herself, even as a traitorous voice whispered doubts in her mind. *'I cannot be a party to his crimes, no matter how much I love him.'*

With a shaky breath, Hetty released her hold on the door and stepped back, her footsteps unnaturally loud in the oppressive stillness of their humble home. She cast a glance around the small living area above her father's undertaker's workshop, taking in the simple furnishings, the worn rug, and the single faded daguerreotype of her mother on the mantle. Everything felt different now, tainted by the knowledge of her father's misdeeds and the harsh words they had exchanged.

'Where do I go from here?' she wondered, a sense of vertigo overtaking her as the reality of her situation sank in. *'What becomes of us, of me, of my father, now that the truth has been laid bare?'*

The muffled sounds of the street below filtered up through the floorboards, a reminder of the world that continued to turn outside their walls. Hetty moved towards the small window, peering out through the threadbare curtains at the cobblestone street below, watching as a group of labourers trudged home in the fading light.

As she stood there, the weight of her confrontation with her father pressed heavily upon her. She had spoken truths that needed to be said, had stood her ground against his denials and excuses. Yet the pain in his eyes, the slump of his shoulders as he finally acknowledged his wrongdoing, haunted her.

A sudden realisation struck her, sending a chill down her spine. The letter, the one that had exposed her father's dealings with the resurrectionists. She had left it on the table in her haste to leave the room. If her father were to find it, to destroy its contents...

'I have to retrieve it,' Hetty decided, steeling herself for another potential confrontation. *'Before it's too late.'*

She gathered her skirts and turned back. For she would not let this secret destroy them, not without ensuring that justice would be served in honour of the dead, and punishment handed out to the guilty parties.

As she moved, the floorboards creaked beneath her feet, a stark reminder of the humble life they led and the wealth they once had—a life that now teetered on the brink of irrevocable change.

Chapter Twenty-Two

Hetty slipped into the alley where Frederick waited, his silhouette barely visible in the weak glow from a distant gas lamp. Her breath formed delicate clouds in the frigid air, dissipating as quickly as they appeared.

"Frederick," she called out softly, her voice laced with urgency.

"Hetty?" His figure emerged from the shadows, concern etching his brow. "What's happened? Your message sounded grave."

She glanced around to ensure they were alone before speaking. "It's my father... I now know he's involved in all of it. The body snatching, the murders, corruption."

"Good heavens." Frederick's eyes widened in shock, and he stepped closer, lowering his voice. "Are you certain?"

"Beyond a doubt," Hetty replied, her own gaze dropping. "I received an anonymous letter confirming his involvement and the constable gave me his signet ring that was found at the scene of a murder. I confronted him; he didn't deny it. I can't speak to him now. Not after knowing what he's done."

Frederick reached out, placing a reassuring hand on her shoulder. "You did what your conscience dictated. That's all anyone can do in such dark times. But there's more at play here."

He withdrew a bundle of papers from his coat pocket, the sound of crinkling parchment breaking the heavy silence between them. Unrolling the pages, he held them out for Hetty to see, his finger tracing over the faded ink.

"Look here," he murmured. "Ledger entries detailing transactions between the resurrectionists and some of Blackstone's most prominent figures. It's a veritable who's who of the town's elite."

Hetty leaned in, squinting at the scrawled handwriting. "Mr Grayson? The town's chief?" Her voice trembled with disbelief. "He visited my father not a fortnight ago. What business could they possibly have together if not this sordid trade?"

"Exactly my thought," Frederick agreed, his expression grim. "Not only that, but Grayson signed off on my father's death confirming it was an accident. I guessed all along it wasn't. If Grayson is entangled in this web, then the corruption runs deeper than we feared."

"Frederick, another name," Hetty whispered urgently, her finger trembling as it hovered above a line in the ledger. "See here—*'Pembroke.'* Surely not the same Pembrokes?"

Frederick leaned closer, his brow furrowing. "The very ones," he confirmed with a solemn nod. "Grace Pembroke's family is entwined in this vile affair. No wonder she has been spreading gossip about you. It has been an attempt to keep you from the truth."

Hetty clenched her fists, the fabric of her modest skirt crinkling under her grasp. "But she's to marry George Carter—the match of the season!" Her voice was laced with disgust and disbelief. "How could she be part of such horror? I'm sure he will not know, there is not a chance he would marry her otherwise."

"Frederick, what are we going to do?" Hetty's eyes met his, reflecting the weight of their discovery.

"We must tread carefully," he advised, rolling up the ledger pages and tucking them back into his pocket. "Power and wealth breed their own kinds of monstrosities," Frederick said, his tone bitter. "We cannot let her continue unchallenged. We must expose her, for all of Blackstone to see."

"Revenge, then," Hetty stated flatly, her resolve hardening like the cobblestones beneath their feet. "For every soul laid bare by their greed."

"Justice, Hetty," corrected Frederick. "Not revenge. We'll make her, Grayson, and the rest of them answer for their deeds."

Their pact hung heavy in the cold night air, a shared determination binding them amidst the shadows.

Suddenly, the sharp clatter of a knocked-over dustbin pierced the silence, echoing off the soot-stained walls. They froze, eyes wide as they searched the darkness. A figure loomed at the entrance of the alley; its form obscured by the swirling mist that seemed to conspire with the secrets of the night.

"Hide," Frederick mouthed, grabbing Hetty's arm and pulling her behind a stack of wooden crates.

They huddled together, barely daring to breathe as the figure's slow, deliberate footsteps approached. Hetty's heart pounded against her

THE DAUGHTER'S ENDURING LOVE

ribcage, each beat a drum call to danger. She could feel Frederick's steady presence at her side, a silent vow of protection.

"Who's there?" The shadowy figure called out, the voice gruff and searching. "Show yourself!"

"Stay quiet," Frederick whispered, his breath warm against her ear.

Time stretched taut as the figure lingered, the threat of discovery hanging over them like a guillotine blade. Then, as if satisfied, the figure retreated, steps fading back into the night.

"Was it one of them, do you think?" Hetty asked, once the danger had passed enough for hushed words.

"Perhaps," Frederick replied, his gaze scanning the alley's exit. "But we can't take any chances. Not now."

"Then we must act swiftly," Hetty concluded, steeling herself for the trials ahead. "Before more shadows come seeking us."

"Frederick, we must split up," Hetty insisted, pulling her shawl tighter against the chill of the pre-dawn air. "I'll blend in at the marketplace; you search the alleys."

He frowned, clearly reluctant. "Hetty, it's dangerous. If they're watching—"

"Then they'll find it harder to watch two sparrows than one," she countered, her blue eyes fierce with determination. "We need more pieces to this puzzle if we're to expose them all."

"Alright," he conceded, his jaw setting firmly. "But be cautious, Hetty. We can't afford any missteps."

"Nor can we afford hesitation," she replied.

They parted with a lingering, charged glance.

Chapter Twenty-Three

The morning sun had just begun to creep over the rooftops of Blackstone as Hetty descended into the thrumming heart of the marketplace.

The cacophony of haggling voices, braying livestock, and clinking coins was a stark contrast to the silent tension of the previous night. Her gaze swept over the stalls, feigning casual interest while searching for signs, hints – anything that could further unravel the web of corruption.

"Miss Morgan, isn't it?" An elderly vendor's voice sliced through her thoughts, as gnarled as the apples he peddled. "A fine morning to you."

"Mr Thorne," she greeted, forcing a smile as she approached his cart. "Indeed, it is. Your apples look particularly ripe today."

"Ah, but it's not fruit that weighs heavy on your mind, lass," he said, eyeing her with a knowing glint. "Word travels fast in Blackstone, especially when whispers of resurrectionists are involved."

Hetty leaned in closer, her heart quickening. "What have you heard, Mr Thorne?"

"More than I'd like," he muttered, casting a wary glance around before continuing. "There's talk of coaches, late at night, going to and from the homes of men who fancy themselves kings of this town."

"Men such as ..." Hetty, hesitated, wondering whether to mention any names. "Mr Grayson?" Hetty prodded gently.

"Perhaps," Thorne replied, his expression unreadable. "But there are others, too. Names that would curdle your blood."

"Tell me, please. It's important."

"Important enough to risk a noose?" he countered, his eyes narrowing slightly. "I've said too much already. But watch the comings and goings, Miss Morgan. And keep an eye on the tides—they bring more than fish to our docks."

"Thank you, Mr Thorne," Hetty whispered, her mind racing with the implications of his words. She dropped a coin into his hand and turned away, her thoughts a maelstrom as she navigated through the crowd.

Chapter Twenty-Four

As dusk settled over the cobblestone streets of London, the costermongers and street sellers wearily wheeled their carts away for the day. Their calloused hands counted out meagre earnings of ha'pennies and farthings, hoping it would be enough to put bread and watery broth on the table for their families.

The air, thick with coal smoke and the day's lingering cries of *'Who'll buy?'*, gradually gave way to the mournful calls of chimney sweeps returning home, their faces blackened with soot. In the deepening shadows, ragged street urchins darted between closing shops

THE DAUGHTER'S ENDURING LOVE 115

and passing carriages, their keen eyes searching for any morsel—a bruised apple, a crust of bread—left behind to fill their empty bellies.

The gas lamps flickered to life, casting a wan glow over the city's stark contrasts of wealth and want as another day in Victorian London drew to a close.

Frederick adjusted the collar of his coat as he strolled through the shadowy lanes of the town, his mind a jumble of ledgers and clandestine whispers. The weight of the secret tucked inside his pocket pressed against him like an accusation.

"Frederick Pritchard!" bellowed a voice from across the street, slicing through the fog. "Hold up there!"

He turned to see Joe Blythe, a burly man with a reputation for gossip as substantial as his frame, striding toward him. Blythe's eyes held a flicker of suspicion that Frederick knew all too well.

"Joe," Frederick greeted, his tone cautious but cordial. "What brings you out on such a bracing evening?"

"More like what's driven you to skulk around at odd hours, eh?" Blythe thrust his hands into his pockets, squinting at Frederick. "I've seen you, Fred. Out late, whisperin' in alleys. You're not yourself these days."

"Blackstone is full of shadows; one must tread carefully," Frederick replied evenly, his gaze never wavering.

"Carefully, or carelessly?" Blythe challenged, leaning forward. "People are talkin', Fred. They say you're mixed up in somethin' dark."

"Talk is cheap, Joe," Frederick retorted, his patience waning. "And I find it best to keep my own counsel."

"Is it Hetty Morgan? She's been seen askin' questions, pokin' her nose where it don't belong," Blythe pressed, his voice lowering to a conspiratorial murmur.

"Hetty is of no concern to you," Frederick said sharply, the protective edge in his voice unmistakable. "She's been through enough without idle tongues wagging."

"Ah, so it is her," Blythe grinned, his eyes gleaming with triumph. "And what would her pa think—"

"Her father thinks only of himself," Frederick cut in, his composure slipping. "Leave Hetty be, Joe. This matter is larger than you know."

"Fine, keep your secrets," Blythe grumbled, stepping back. "But remember, even walls have ears around 'ere."

"Indeed they do," Frederick agreed, watching Blythe retreat into the mist before turning towards home.

Beatrice was waiting by the hearth when he arrived home, her brow creased with worry. "Frederick, where have you been? It's nearly supper."

"Out," he answered, removing his coat and revealing the ledger. "There's much to discuss, ma. But first, we need to offer sanctuary."

"Sanctuary?" Beatrice echoed, puzzled.

"Hetty cannot go back to her father's house. It's not safe," Frederick explained, his words urgent. "She has nowhere else to turn."

"Then she'll stay with us," Beatrice declared without hesitation, her loyalty as solid as the earth itself. "We'll make room. She's family."

"Thank you, ma," Frederick sighed, relief softening his features. "I knew I could count on you."

"Always, dear son, always," Beatrice smiled, her resolve firm. "Now come, let's eat. We'll need our strength for what lies ahead."

As they settled at the table, there was a knock at the door.

"Hetty, come in, come in out of that cold," Beatrice called, ushering the young woman through the door.

Hetty followed Frederick into the kitchen where a fire crackled merrily, its warmth a stark contrast to the chill that had settled in her bones. As she removed her damp shawl, her eyes met Frederick's, a silent understanding passing between them.

Beatrice's brow furrowed as she turned to Hetty, concern etching lines around her kind eyes. "What is it, dear? You look as though you've seen a ghost."

Hetty drew in a shivering breath, the flickering firelight casting dancing shadows across her pale face. Her voice quavered, but she pressed on. "My father and I, our lives are in danger."

"Good heavens!" Beatrice gasped, reaching out to clasp Hetty's trembling hands. "What do you mean, child?"

"The resurrectionists," Hetty continued, her eyes glistening with unshed tears. "If the murders stopped—if my father ceased providing those bodies—they would turn on us. The web of corruption extends far beyond what we imagined."

Beatrice's face paled, her grip on Hetty's hands tightening. "Oh, my dear girl. What a terrible burden you carry." She glanced at her son, then back to Hetty. "What will you do?"

Another sharp knock at the door sliced through the conversation, not giving Hetty time to respond.

Frederick stood swiftly, his chair scraping against the wood floor. "Who could that be at this late hour?" he asked as he moved toward the door. "Stay here," Frederick instructed, casting a protective glance over his shoulder before he disappeared into the hallway.

Hetty sat frozen, listening intently. The fear that gripped her was not just for her own safety, but for the tenuous thread of hope she held for a life with George.

Frederick opened the door to a gust of night air that carried in the cold and a faint scent of lilac. Grace Pembroke stood on the doorstep, her blonde hair swept up under a velvet bonnet and her green eyes wide with urgency. She stepped into the candlelit room without invitation, the hem of her fine dress whispering against the floorboards.

"Beatrice, Hetty, Frederick," she began, her voice a blend of fear and determination. "I've come because I must warn you—my family's name... it's been found in your ledger. Linked to those vile resurrectionists."

Hetty rose slowly from her chair, her blue eyes fixed upon Grace's face, searching for truth amidst the trepidation. "And how did you come by this knowledge?" she asked, the measured tone of her inquiry betraying none of the turmoil that churned within her.

"It matters not," Grace dismissed with a flick of her wrist. "What is imperative is that you understand the gravity of the situation. My reputation, my engagement to George—it all stands on the precipice of ruin."

"Your engagement?" Hetty echoed, the mention of George's name causing her heart to stutter. "If you are so concerned for your standing, Miss Pembroke, then perhaps it is time you told your family to cease their dealings. Or is your social stature worth more than your conscience? Perhaps I should inform your social circle and George of your family dealings if you're not willing to tell the truth?"

Grace's lips pressed together, forming a tight line. "You wouldn't dare."

"Wouldn't I?" Hetty's voice gained strength as she took a step forward. "Your family's misgivings could shatter your future with George. Is that a risk you are willing to take?"

"Hetty," Frederick interjected, his brow furrowed in concern. "Perhaps we should—"

"Silence," snapped Grace, her gaze flinty as she addressed Hetty. "You know not the power my family wields. But very well, I shall see what can be done."

"See that you do," Hetty replied, though as Grace swept from the room, her resolve wavered. She turned to Frederick, her expression fraught with confusion. "Who has told her? Who else knows of our discoveries?"

"Hetty, we've been careful," Frederick assured her, taking her hands in his. "But we must consider that someone close to us might be watching."

"Watching... and waiting," Hetty murmured. Her mind raced, suspicion clouding her thoughts. The ledger was supposed to be their secret weapon, yet now it seemed to wield its own threat—a danger that extended beyond the pages and into the very fabric of their trust.

"Trust no one, Hetty," Frederick said softly, echoing her inner fears. "Not until we uncover the full extent of this corruption."

'*Trust no one,*' she repeated, as she felt the stirrings of despair.

Chapter Twenty-Five

George Carter paced the length of the living room, the heels of his polished boots clicking against the hardwood floor. Robert, his brother sat behind their father's mahogany desk. The flickering light from the fire casting warm glows on their faces.

"Robert," he began, pausing to look into the flames before turning his earnest brown eyes toward him. "I find myself in a rather perplexing situation."

"I think I know what this is about, but go on," he encouraged, sensing the turmoil that gripped his older brother.

THE DAUGHTER'S ENDURING LOVE 121

"It's Hetty," he confessed, the words tumbling out in a rush. "My mind is fraught with thoughts of her at all hours. Yet, I am acutely aware of the expectations laid upon me."

"Expectations can be suffocating as we have discussed before, George, even to people like us who have been brought up surrounded by luxury and wealth, his voice laced with empathy.

He nodded, running a hand through his dark hair—a rare gesture that betrayed his inner conflict. "Society itself has a role set out for us, but do we have of follow it? What if it doesn't include someone like Hetty?"

"Then you have to do what's right, even if it goes against everything that our parents want for us. And I guarantee that Hetty will not be included in their plans for you."

"I suppose to defy such norms would bring dishonour, not just to me, but to my entire lineage," George's voice cracked slightly, revealing the depth of his anxiety.

"Is it dishonourable to follow one's heart though brother?" What do we have if we don't have love? Oil paintings, rugs, ornaments? And what value would they hold in our hearts? None!" Robert stood up and walked over to the large window. He put his hands in his pockets as he looked out onto the manicured lawn and box hedged pathway as far as his eyes could see.

"Perhaps not. But the repercussions..." A tremble coursed through his words as he spoke. "I fear them, Robert. The disappointment I would cast upon our family, the whispers behind closed doors, the scornful gazes—it feels insurmountable."

"George," Robert said, walking over to his brother and reaching out to place a reassuring hand on his arm, "your heart is kind and your intentions are pure. Surely those who truly care for you would want your happiness above all else?"

"Would they?" He met his gaze, vulnerability etched across his features. "Or would they see it as selfishness? As folly?"

"I would understand, I would stand by you. But may I ask, does Hetty return these feelings that have you so conflicted?"

"I believe she might," he admitted, a hint of hope flickering amidst the worry. "But even the possibility of our union seems like a distant dream."

"Sometimes," Robert said with a soft smile, "the most distant dreams are the ones most worth reaching for."

George took a deep breath, as if drawing strength from her words. "I cannot escape the fact that my decisions will ripple far beyond my own life. It's a burden I carry each day."

"Then allow me to help you shoulder that burden, George. You need not face these choices alone." His tone was steadfast, his intent clear—to support him no matter the cost.

"Thank you, Robert. I do not know what I would do without your counsel," he said, the gratitude in his eyes genuine.

"Just promise me this," he added, his expression serious yet kind, "that you will consider your happiness."

George nodded solemnly. "I promise."

"Look, brother. You know I lost my one true love. I did not express myself fully to her for fear of repercussions from Father. I was too worried that he would discount me from the estate, to reject me from the family. But no amount of exclusion is worse than not being with someone you love with all of your heart. No matter what the cost, you must follow what you desire and pursue who you truly believe you want to spend the rest of your life with." Robert tried desperately to blink the acidic tears from his eyes.

"Robert, one day you will find someone equally a beautiful, loving, and charismatic lady as Charlotte was, I promise you. Just be patient."

"I appreciate your positivity, George, I will hold it within me until that day arrives."

As the conversation waned, the weight of George's internal struggle lingered in the air.

Chapter Twenty-Six

"Frederick, look at this," Hetty's voice cut through the silence of the room like a sharp blade as she held out a tattered piece of paper with trembling hands. The gaslight flickered above them, casting an eerie glow over the parchment that seemed to hold secrets too grim for daylight.

Frederick leaned closer, his hazel eyes scanning the words hastily scrawled across the surface. "This definitely implicates the Pembrokes in the murders, doesn't it?"

Hetty nodded, the resolve in her blue eyes unwavering despite the gravity of their discovery. "I've cross-referenced the handwriting with the letters sent to the anatomy schools. It's definitely Grace's uncle."

The implications were immediate and terrifying. To accuse a family as powerful as the Pembrokes could mean ruin, or worse, retribution. Yet, the injustice of it all—the innocent lives lost—stoked a fire within Hetty that not even the chill creeping through the ill-fitting window panes could extinguish.

"Then we need to tread carefully," Frederick said, running a hand through his tousled brown hair. "Because if we're wrong ..."

"We're not wrong," Hetty interjected, her spirit undeterred. "But if word of this gets out before we can prove it, Grace will make sure our reputations are destroyed."

"Hetty," Frederick began, his tone both gentle and firm, "you know what this means for your family, right?"

She cut him off with a wave of her hand, her posture stiffening in defiance. "I'm well aware. But how can I stand by while they use their influence to cover up such heinous crimes?"

Frederick sighed, recognising the determined tilt of her chin—a clear sign that Hetty Morgan would not be swayed from what she considered just.

"Alright then," he conceded, "we'll need a plan."

"Let them come," Hetty declared, her voice rising with conviction. "For too long have those like us borne the cost of their corruption. No more. I'm sure they are setting my father up in these murders."

"But I thought your father had confessed, Hetty? I don't understand."

"Neither do I fully, but I have a feeling my father has confessed to save his life. The resurrectionists must be using him as a way for covering up for themselves. The resurrectionists pay him money to collect more bodies and extra shillings if he makes false ledgers in his books. Then it looks as if he is the one orchestrating the whole operation." Hetty looked pensively out of the window.

"He is being used, Hetty. We must try and clear his name, the alternative is too unimaginable. I know all too well how it feels to lose a father," Frederick said, blinking back tears.

"But how do I clear my father's name? I can live with …" she hesitated. "I can live without George if it means my father breaking free from these dreadful people," she sighed as she gazed towards the floor.

"No, you couldn't. Your feelings for George are very clear and anyone would be a fool if they hadn't noticed. We must prove Grace's family's dealings with the resurrection gang and the murders."

"Then we must hope that George will turn against Grace and no longer marry her. I can't see him wanting to be with a woman who has connections to the atrocities happening in the town, can you?"

"No, I can't. It will cause implications for his relationship with his family too, especially if his father is involved."

"Oh, Frederick, this is terrible. Families will be torn apart, people's feelings will be destroyed, relationships tethered."

"I agree, Hetty, but the alternative is that the true culprits are never exposed, the resurrectionists continue to blackmail your father, and the murders keep rising."

Hetty knew Frederick was right. She bit her bottom lip whilst thinking about the next move. She looked up at Frederick with determination in her eyes. "We need to allow George to find out for himself, don't force the evidence or findings on him, otherwise it will look as if I am trying to pull him away from Grace."

"But you are trying to pull him away, Hetty."

"I know, but I don't want him to think it is contrived in any way."

"So, we must let people know that Grace's family is involved but do it anonymously. Print leaflets, post them through doors, whisper in people's ears. That way, George will eventually find out and hopefully fall into your arms."

"I think you might be right. But they will know I'm involved, it's too obvious," she said, pacing the room. "It will soon be the town fete, no doubt the gossip mongers will be talking about nothing except George and Grace's engagement. But if we tell everyone about her family dealings before then, maybe the gossip will switch to one of slander on the Pembrokes," a beaming smile spread across Hetty's face.

"I've just had a thought, Hetty. Do you not think all of this will affect George too? His work, his patients, his social standing?"

"I did consider that," Hetty replied, her eyes shining with conviction. "But when people see the evidence with no mention of George's name anywhere, they will be so engrossed in the dealings of the resurrectionists and who is guilty, they won't be interested in him. Remember, Frederick, people are fickle and they move on quickly to the next misgivings and gossip between social circles," she said, pacing the room. "Besides, George's reputation in this town is unassailable. He's adored for his work with patients, his kindness to the poor, and his unwavering dedication to healing. If anything, learning of the Pembrokes' involvement might only serve to cast George in an even more favourable light – the good doctor who narrowly escaped being ensnared by such a corrupt family. No, Frederick, I'm certain that George's standing will remain untarnished, perhaps even elevated, once the truth comes to light."

"In which case we must hurry. The fete starts in two days, which means the news of the engagement will be imminent and we have work to do."

Hetty clasped her hands together and brought them to her mouth, already plotting about how the gossip could be spread far and wide. '*It will be worth it,*' she mused. '*Anything to marry George Carter,*' she pulled her shawl around her and left Fredrick's home.

Chapter Twenty-Seven

The heaviness in Hetty's heart had been harbouring for what felt like days. She missed her father terribly, even though she was the one to leave. She had to see him.

As she neared her father's house, she heard footsteps behind her. Hetty turned around but couldn't see anything because of the mist and drizzle. There was nothing but shadows playing tricks with her mind against the orange glow of the oil lamps that cast hardly any brightness on the streets.

As she turned to look ahead, she noticed a shadowy figure outside her father's parlour. As she got closer, he thrust a scrap of paper into her hand then ran off into the dark. Hetty's fingers trembled as she read the words that scrawled across it like poison, each letter a fang sinking into her flesh.

'Your secrets are not so well kept, Miss Morgan. Blackstone whispers of your dark dealings and the company you keep. I urge you to keep the findings to yourself or it may be your pa that ends up behind bars, or worse, left hanging from the rafters with his eyes bulging and his tongue lolling out of his mouth. What a sight that would be. I promise you, stay away or face the punishment for spreading the scandal.'

"Miss Morgan," a voice called from behind.

Hetty jerked her head quickly, surprised at the voice in the darkness. She turned to find Mrs Haversham, her father's neighbour, eyeing her with a mixture of curiosity and disdain. "I hear you've been consorting with the doctor, that Carter boy. And they say you're meddling where you oughtn't. Is there truth to these mutterings?"

Hetty drew herself up, her resolve hardening like the cobble beneath her feet. "Good evening, Mrs Haversham. Rumours are the currency of the bored and the malicious. I suggest you invest more wisely. All I'm doing is finding the truth so we can all rest easy and sleep safe in our beds at night. I'm certain if it was one of your lads who had been murdered by the resurrectionists, you would want to know what was going on in this town."

"Indeed," the older woman replied with a sceptical arch of her brow. "Well, just remember that mud clings most tenaciously to those who tread in unsavoury places. If what you're sayin' about these Pembrokes is true, I'll support you. If it's not ... then be warned." With a huff, she bustled away, leaving Hetty alone with the echo of her words.

"But how—?" Hetty didn't get a chance to finish her words. *'How do you know what my findings are?'* she thought to herself. Her eyes lifted to the dark sky above, where crows circled like dark omens.

THE DAUGHTER'S ENDURING LOVE 131

She felt the weight of Grace's influence pressing down upon her, an invisible hand trying to crush her spirit. But was it Grace trying to silence the rumours and gossip, or was it someone closer to home?

"Hetty?" The voice was gentle, familiar.

Hetty startled in the dark. "Did you follow me home?" Hetty asked her friend.

"Purely to make sure you made it back safely," Frederick said.

"Frederick," she greeted him, forcing a smile. "I've had a note, a threatening one."

"Pay them no heed," he said, coming to stand beside her. "People who write those letters are born of fear and ignorance."

"Perhaps," she sighed. "But fear and ignorance can do much harm. And when it bears the mark of the Pembrokes..." Her voice trailed off.

"Grace has made certain of that," Frederick agreed, his tone grim. "She wields her family's name like a sword, cutting down anyone who dares challenge her."

Hetty nodded, folding her arms against the chill that had nothing to do with the weather. She could feel the eyes of the town on her, measuring her worth and finding it wanting. In their gaze, she was not Hetty Morgan, a woman of strength and conviction; she was the undertaker's daughter, tainted by trade with the dead and now tarnished by association with high society's golden boy.

"Goodnight, Frederick, I'm going to see my father," she said, pulling the shawl tighter around her.

"Goodnight, Hetty, stay safe," he said, before turning around and walking away.

Chapter Twenty-Eight

The door creaked open, and George Carter stepped across the threshold. His silhouette, outlined by the fading light of dusk, hesitated just inside the room as if gathering the strength to face what lay within.

"George," Hetty murmured, her voice barely above a whisper but laden with surprise. She rose from her chair by the fireplace, where she had been hunched over a tangle of notes and newspaper clippings.

"Forgive my intrusion, Hetty." His words stumbled slightly, betraying the turmoil beneath his composed exterior. "I find myself in need of your counsel."

THE DAUGHTER'S ENDURING LOVE 133

Hetty glanced at him, noting the unusual disarray of his hair and the slight tremor in his hands. "Of course," she said, motioning towards the seat opposite hers. "I was just reading whilst waiting for my father, I need to see him. Please, sit."

He declined with a shake of his head, choosing instead to pace before the hearth. The flickering flames cast dancing shadows across his features, accentuating the earnestness in his eyes. "It's about... It's about my feelings for you," he confessed, halting his stride to meet her gaze directly.

Her heart skipped a beat, and her breath caught in her throat. "Your feelings?" she echoed faintly, taking a hesitant step toward him.

"Yes," he continued, the vulnerability creeping into his voice. "I've tried to deny them, to bury them beneath duty and expectation, but they persist—stronger, even, than my fear of disappointing my family."

"George," Hetty stood up and reached out, her fingertips brushing against his sleeve before she quickly withdrew her hand, suddenly aware of the impropriety. Their eyes locked, and for a moment, time seemed to stand still. She saw the conflict raging within him, mirrored by her own inner battle.

"Hetty, I—" George leaned forward, his breath mingling with hers, his intent clear in the softening of his expression.

She could feel the warmth radiating from his body, the closeness threatening to unravel her composure. Her own desire surged forward, an almost magnetic pull drawing her to close the gap between them.

But as their lips hovered mere inches apart, Hetty's mind screamed with warnings. She remembered the note from Grace—the sharp sting of betrayal—and the precarious nature of their situation. With a strength she hadn't known she possessed, Hetty took a step back, putting distance between them once more.

"George," she began again, steadying her voice, though it wavered with emotion. "We must be careful. I cannot afford to have my heart broken, not when so much is at stake."

"Nor can I," he conceded, his voice laced with pain. "I understand, truly." He straightened, the moment of weakness passing as he donned the familiar armour of propriety.

"Then we agree," Hetty stated, despite the ache that hollowed her chest.

"Agree on what?"

"To stay apart."

"I don't know if I can," George said, reaching out. "We must find a way to be together, I cannot marry Grace."

"And I cannot see you marry her, it would break my heart, and I fear living alone for the rest of my life, because I don't want anyone else. My heart and soul burn for you in a way that only you can dampen the flames."

"In which case we must find a way to spend the rest of our lives together without hurting anybody's feelings."

"I think I have a way for us to do that, George," Hetty said, looking pensive at the tall, dark, and delectable physician standing in front of her."

"And how would you do that?"

"Promise you will hear what I have to say?"

"Of course, Hetty. Your words mean more to me than anything."

"I have found evidence that implicates Grace's family in the recent resurrectionist gang and murders."

George gasped. "Grace's family? But how? And why would they be involved?"

"I don't know that right now. All I have found is copies of letters to the physicians in handwriting that match Grace's Uncle's writing. I found letters he had sent to the resurrectionists instructing them to murder, and offering good money for it too."

"Where did you get those, Hetty? And how is that going to help us be together?"

Hetty bit her bottom lip. For a moment, she sensed George was angry at her. "I found them in my father's ledger. I know they are trying to blame him for the murders, but he is in so much debt, he won't stand up for himself in fear of what they might do to him. To me."

"Why do you think your father has them?"

"I think the gang are forcing him to keep them so if they are found, he will get the blame."

George looked startled and paced the floor. He took a deep breath in. "But, Hetty, I still don't see what you have found will help us."

"I am going to tell everyone about the Pembrokes' dealings. The town fete is happening in a couple of days. I hope for the most intent gossip mongers in the town, that they will talk of nothing but how dreadful and backhanded the Pembrokes are. Then, naturally you will hear the gossip and use it as a reason to call the engagement off." Hetty looked up at her one true love and couldn't decide if she had said too much and ruined her chances.

George stopped pacing and looked at Hetty. He shook his head and blinked slowly. "How could this have happened? How could I have not noticed what Grace ... what she was involved with? Damn her!" He shouted, before thumping the wall. He looked down at his bleeding knuckles.

"George! I'm sorry," Hetty said, rushing over to him and lifting his hand. She wet her thumb and wiped the blood away. "Here, come and sit me down, let me dress that for you." Hetty led George over to the armchair by the fire.

George allowed himself to be guided by the most beautiful, caring woman he had ever met. He had no intention of allowing her to slip away. He had to do something. George sat back in the chair, his knees slightly apart, and focussed on Hetty's face, which was highlighted by the flames of the fire. He watched her tenderly and carefully wrap a dressing around his knuckles.

"Thank you," he whispered. "I didn't mean to do that, I've never lashed out before."

"I know," she said.

"Hetty, I don't want to see you get hurt. If what you tell me is true about the Pembrokes, they could hurt you."

"I would do anything for you, I would ... die for you," she said. "Oh, I'm sorry, that was ... that was too much, too soon."

"No, no it wasn't." George took hold of her hand and kissed it gently. "You must do what you said and I promise I will watch you every step of the way. Tomorrow I will ask Grace to marry me and act as normal. I will pretend I haven't heard anything, and say that she means everything to me."

Hetty's heart skipped a couple of beats. "Oh," she said disappointingly.

"It's just for now," George said, lifting her face with a finger. He stroked her chin and looked into her eyes. "All the time I will be thinking of you. Then when I hear the gossip about the Pembrokes, I will act shocked and confused and call off the engagement."

"Very well then, that's what we must do. For the sake of outing the truth, clearing my father's name, and spending the rest of our lives together."

"Yes, we must. And no doubt my family will be aghast when they hear what the Pembroke's have done. They are dear friends of my family, but they won't want to be involved with them when they hear the truth."

"George, can I ask, before you leave," Hetty whispered, the glow from the fire danced across her face, revealing the depth of her concern. "The bodies taken from their graves, it's an abomination. And now there's talk of legislation to stop these *'resurrectionists,'* but will it be enough?"

He stood by the window, his silhouette outlined against the darkening sky of Blackstone. "I've heard of it," he replied, his voice measured but thick with emotion. "They seek to regulate the trade of cadavers for medical research, to put an end to this gruesome business."

"Regulate, yes, but at what cost?" Hetty turned to him, her eyes alight with a fire that matched the hearth. "It's justice for the dead we seek, George. But what of the living? Those who must bear the burden of these crimes?"

George turned from the window, his gaze settling on her with a weight that spoke volumes. "As a physician, my family expects me to dismiss these matters as unseemly," he confessed, his hands clasped behind his back in a sign of restraint. "But I cannot. Not when it touches my heart."

"My findings could change everything, not just for us, but for all of Blackstone. They will change everything, George, but I will feel safe with you by my side."

"And I with you, Hetty. Now, I must go and prepare myself for what is to happen." He lifted Hetty's hand once more and kissed it tenderly.

"Goodnight, George." She watched him leave, the click of the door echoing through the quiet room like the closing of a book—a chapter of their lives left unwritten.

Chapter Twenty-Nine

The Town Hall of Blackstone stood resplendent in the fading light of the day, its weathered stone facade adorned with bunting and garlands for the annual harvest fete. The air hummed with excitement as the town's residents gathered inside to celebrate.

Hetty stood at the periphery of the crowd, her gloved hands clasped tightly before her. Her emerald silk gown, which seemed to shine beneath the gas lamps and candles, was striking, and caught the attention of many. Ladies turned their husband's wandering eyes away from the sight before them. And although Hetty Morgan exuded confidence within the room, her eyes darted nervously about the assembly, searching for one face in particular.

As if summoned by her thoughts, Grace Pembroke swept into view, a vision in lavender taffeta. Her golden curls bounced with each step, and her tinkling laughter carried across the murmur of the crowd. On her arm, looking every inch the proud fiancé, was Dr George Carter.

Hetty's heart constricted at the sight. The memory of George's visit to her sitting room burned fresh in her mind. His confession of feelings, the almost kiss that still haunted her dreams, and the weight of the secrets that now lay between them.

"Miss Morgan!" A booming voice startled Hetty from her reverie. "How delightful to see you here tonight."

She turned to find Mr Bartholomew Finch, the portly owner of Blackstone's most prestigious haberdashery, beaming at her. "Good evening, Mr Finch," she replied, forcing a smile. "I trust you're well?"

"Never better, my dear, never better!" He patted his considerable belly. "Though I daresay Mrs Finch will have my hide if I overindulge in Mrs Holloway's famous apple tarts again this year."

Hetty laughed politely, her eyes still tracking Grace and George as they made their way through the crowd. "I'm sure Mrs Finch would understand the temptation. The harvest fete comes but once a year, after all."

"Too true, too true!" Mr Finch agreed heartily. "Speaking of once-in-a-lifetime events, have you heard the news? Young Dr Carter has finally taken the plunge! Engaged to Miss Pembroke, of all people. Quite the catch, wouldn't you say?"

Hetty's smile faltered for just a moment before she recovered. "Indeed, Mr Finch. They make a striking couple."

"That they do, that they do." Mr Finch leaned in conspiratorially. "Though between you and me, Miss Morgan, I always thought you and the good doctor might... Well, I saw you around in the town walking together. But never mind an old man's ramblings. Will you excuse me? I see Mrs Holloway setting out those tarts, and I must stake my claim before they vanish!"

As Mr Finch waddled away, Hetty took a steadying breath. She had known this moment would come, had steeled herself for it, but the reality of seeing George and Grace together, accepting congratulations and basking in the approval of Blackstone society, was almost more than she could bear.

Across the room, Grace caught Hetty's eye and raised a perfectly arched eyebrow. With a whisper to George, she disentangled herself from his arm and glided towards Hetty, her face a mask of saccharine sweetness.

"Hetty, darling!" Grace cooed as she approached. "How lovely to see you. I was beginning to think you might not come."

Hetty straightened her spine, meeting Grace's gaze with a steel of her own. "I wouldn't miss the harvest fete for the world, Grace. It's such an important event for the town."

"Of course, of course," Grace agreed, her voice dripping with false sincerity. "And I'm so glad you're here to share in my happiness. George and I are simply overwhelmed by everyone's well-wishes."

Hetty's fingers twitched, longing to ball into fists. Instead, she plastered on a smile that didn't quite reach her eyes. "Might I have a word with you in private, Grace? There's a matter I'd like to discuss."

A flicker of uncertainty passed over Grace's features before her mask of composure slid back into place. "Certainly, dear. Shall we step out onto the terrace? The air in here is becoming quite stifling."

The two women made their way through the crowded hall, nodding politely to acquaintances as they passed. Hetty could feel George's eyes on her back, but she didn't dare turn to meet his gaze.

Once outside, the cool early evening air provided little relief from the tension that crackled between them.

Grace turned, her simpering smile replaced by a look of cool disdain. "Well, Hetty? What is so important that you must drag me away from my adoring public?"

Hetty's voice was low and steady when she spoke. "I'm giving you one last chance, Grace. Tell George the truth about your family's involvement with the resurrectionists and the murders, or I will."

Grace's eyes widened for a fraction of a second before narrowing dangerously. "I'm sure I don't know what you're talking about, Hetty dear. Perhaps the excitement of the evening has addled your wits?"

"Don't play coy with me," Hetty hissed, taking a step closer. "I have evidence, Grace. Letters in your uncle's hand, detailing instructions to the gang. How much they were to be paid for each... acquisition."

The colour drained from Grace's face, but her voice remained steady. "You're bluffing. You couldn't possibly—"

"I found them," Hetty pressed on, her heart pounding. "Your family has been using my father, threatening him, trying to pin the blame on an innocent man. But I won't let that happen. I won't let you destroy my father, or George, or this town."

Grace's facade cracked, revealing a glimpse of the desperation beneath. "You don't understand, Hetty. My family... we had no choice. The advancements in medical science, the need for specimens. It's all for the greater good."

"The greater good?" Hetty's voice rose, trembling with anger. "Is that what you tell yourself to justify murder? To sleep at night knowing that families are being torn apart, graves desecrated?"

"Keep your voice down!" Grace hissed, glancing nervously over her shoulder at the open doors of the hall. "You have no idea what you're meddling with, Hetty. If you breathe a word of this to anyone, I'll—"

"You'll what?" Hetty challenged, standing her ground. "Threaten me like you've threatened my father? I'm not afraid of you, Grace. Not anymore."

For a long moment, the two women stared at each other, the sounds of laughter and music from inside the hall a stark contrast to the tension on the terrace. Finally, Grace spoke, her voice barely above a whisper.

"What do you want from me, Hetty? To confess all to George? To ruin my family's name, our standing in society?"

Hetty's expression softened slightly. "I want you to do the right thing, Grace. For once in your life, think of someone other than yourself. George deserves to know the truth about the family he's marrying into. And the victims... they deserve justice."

Grace's shoulders sagged, the fight seeming to drain out of her. "And if I refuse?"

"Then I'll have no choice but to tell George myself," Hetty said firmly. "And not just George. The authorities, the newspapers... everyone will know what your family has done."

Grace's eyes flashed with a mixture of fear and anger. "You wouldn't dare."

"Try me," Hetty replied, her voice steel. "You have until the end of the fete, Grace. Make your choice."

With that, Hetty turned on her heel and strode back into the hall, leaving Grace alone on the terrace, her carefully constructed world teetering on the brink of collapse.

Inside, the festivities continued unabated, oblivious to the storm brewing just beyond the walls. Hetty made her way through the crowd, accepting a glass of punch from a passing waiter and taking a fortifying sip. Her confrontation with Grace had left her shaken, but resolute. Whatever came next, she knew she had done the right thing.

As the evening wore on, Hetty found herself drawn into conversations with various townsfolk, all eager to discuss the latest gossip and speculate on the coming winter. She smiled and nodded in all the right places, but her mind was elsewhere, watching the clock and wondering if Grace would make good on her ultimatum.

It was nearing midnight when Hetty felt a presence at her elbow. She turned, expecting to find another well-wisher or perhaps Mr Finch returning from his tart-induced stupor. Instead, she found herself face to face with George Carter.

"Miss Morgan," he said softly, his eyes searching hers. "Might I have a word?"

Hetty's heart leapt into her throat. She nodded, not trusting her voice, and allowed George to guide her towards a quiet corner of the hall. As they walked, she could feel the eyes of the other guests upon them, no doubt wondering at the impropriety of the newly engaged doctor seeking out a private audience with another young woman.

When they were as alone as they could be in such a crowded space, George leaned in close, his breath warm against her ear. "Hetty, I... I need to speak with you. It's urgent."

She looked up at him, noting the worry lines etched across his brow, the tightness around his eyes. "What is it, George? Has something happened?"

He glanced around nervously before meeting her gaze once more. "Not here. Can you meet me at the old willow by the river? In an hour?"

Hetty's mind raced. The old willow had been their secret meeting place a couple of weeks ago where they had shared dreams. To meet there now, in the dead of night... it was beyond improper. And yet...

"George, I don't think—"

"Please, Hetty," he interrupted, his voice low and urgent. "I wouldn't ask if it wasn't important. There's something you need to know."

She searched his face, seeing the conflict, the fear, and something else... something that made her heart skip a beat. Slowly, almost imperceptibly, she nodded.

Relief washed over George's features. He squeezed her hand briefly before stepping back. "Thank you," he whispered. "One hour."

As he melted back into the crowd, Hetty stood rooted to the spot, her mind whirling. What could be so urgent that George would risk both their reputations for a clandestine meeting? Had Grace confessed? Or was there something else, something even more earth-shattering, waiting to be revealed?

The clock on the wall ticked steadily onwards, each second bringing her closer to a moment that she sensed would change everything. As the revellers around her laughed and danced, blissfully unaware of the secrets and lies swirling in their midst, Hetty made her decision.

In one hour, she would meet George by the old willow next to the river. And whatever truths were waiting to be unveiled in the dark of night, she would face them head-on. For better or for worse, the fate of Blackstone – and her own heart – hung in the balance.

With a deep breath, Hetty squared her shoulders and rejoined the party, counting down the minutes until she could slip away into the night. The harvest fete continued around her, a swirl of colour and sound, but for Hetty Hartley, the real drama was yet to unfold.

As the grandfather clock in the corner struck the hour, Hetty made her excuses and slipped out of the Town Hall. The night air was crisp, carrying with it the scent of fallen leaves and coal.

The old willow tree loomed before her, its drooping branches creating a curtain of shadow by the riverbank. As she approached, a figure emerged from behind the trunk, and Hetty's breath caught in her throat.

"George," she whispered, coming to a stop just out of arm's reach. "What's happened? Why all this secrecy?"

He stepped closer, his face half-hidden in shadow. "Hetty, tell me, I thought there was going to be gossip about the Pembroke's family. I've heard nothing. How on earth am I going to break the engagement off for Grace and her family being involved with the resurrectionists and murders if I haven't heard about it amongst the gossip."

Hetty frowned. "George, forgive me, but I thought I was doing the right thing. I had the leaflets printed, and I wrote the letters to put through letterboxes. I wanted everyone to know about the Pembrokes, but then I thought, maybe Grace deserves a chance."

"But, Hetty, what do you mean?" George looked confused.

"Hear me out, George. I didn't think it would put me in a good light spreading rumours and gossip, particularly if we are going to marry. I thought it best for Grace to tell you herself. That way, neither of us are seen as the instigators. I suppose ... well I suppose it avoids Grace being tarnished as much as she could be if everybody knew."

"Oh, Hetty. You are thoughtful. You are aware of the Pembrokes' involvement, but you still choose to tread lightly."

"I want justice, George, but I don't see the point in destroying lives where it's not warranted. Grace might be involved, but not directly. She isn't involved in stealing bodies, and she hasn't got the heart to commit murder. Why implicate her when the only reason I would be doing that is because I want you?"

George stepped closer to Hetty and took her hands in his. He brought them up to his mouth and kissed her fingers. "Very well, in which case we must force Grace to tell me privately, and I will call off the engagement."

"I know how to coerce her into doing that."

"You do?"

Hetty nodded. "Follow me," she said, walking off in the direction of the town hall.

Chapter Thirty

⁓⁓⧫⁓⁓

"George! Where have you—?" Grace stopped talking when she saw Hetty standing behind her fiancé. Her cheeks turned pink, and she felt her blood run cold. "You little— what have you said?"

"Nothing, that's up to you, Grace," Hetty said. "Why don't the three of us go and talk?"

George, Grace, and Hetty entered an empty room. Guests and town folk stared after them, wondering what could possibly be occurring on a night like this. But not Beatrice and Frederick, who stood in the corner of the room, smiling.

"Hetty has orchestrated this perfectly, don't you think, Ma?"

"Yes, she has. And if she wasn't so wrapped up in the physician, she would have made you a wonderful wife."

Frederick remained silent, for he knew his ma was right, but Hetty had made her feelings about George perfectly clear.

"Grace, tell me."

"Tell you what, George?" Grace said, when Hetty had closed the door behind them.

"I want to know if it's true."

Grace gulped down the ball of emotion sitting in the back of her throat. Her bottom lip quivered. "George, please, let me explain. I knew nothing about it. This was all my uncle's doing. He was approached and asked for more bodies. He didn't want to do it himself, so he paid the resurrectionists for more bodies. They took to murder, and I swear I didn't know."

"Did you honestly think I could marry you being connected to filth? What would my family say?" George's eyes turned dark, he stared at the woman he once loved with venom on his tongue. "Why didn't you tell me from the start? It could have saved me from heartache. I can't be associated with you, Grace. The engagement is off!"

"What do you mean? George, you're scaring me."

"Exactly what I said. I can't marry you, Grace. Your connection to what has been going on in the town is simply unacceptable. I won't be connected with it." George stared at Grace for a moment, acknowledging the tears in her eyes. Then he turned around and walked out of the room, slamming the door behind him.

"What have you done?"

Hetty could feel the spittle from Grace's mouth on her face. She moved her head back slightly.

"I will never ever forgive you for this, do you hear me?"

"And I will never forgive you for implicating my father. The Pembrokes almost destroyed him," Hetty responded. "I found the letters to the resurrectionists instructing the murders, I'm assuming they were planted there to implicate him to take the attention away from the Pembrokes."

"Hetty, I would never do such a thing."

"Maybe not, but you are still involved. And I will never forgive you."

Hetty walked out of the room, leaving Grace to fall to the floor, her lilac taffeta circling around her whilst she shed tears of sorrow of what was to come of her life now her love was gone forever.

Chapter Thirty-One

The Carter family's grand manor house loomed before George as he approached, its imposing façade a stark reminder of the weight of expectations that had always rested upon his shoulders. The events of the fete still swirled in his mind, a tempest of emotions threatening to overwhelm him. As he reached for the brass door knocker, George took a steadying breath, steeling himself for the confrontation to come.

The door swung open, revealing Simmons, the family's long-serving butler. "Good evening, Dr Carter," he intoned, his face a mask of polite indifference. "The family is gathered in the drawing room. Shall I announce you?"

George shook his head, removing his hat and coat. "No need, Simmons. Thank you."

As he made his way through the familiar halls, George's steps faltered. The portraits of Carter ancestors seemed to watch him with judging eyes, their painted gazes a silent reminder of the family legacy he was about to upend. The murmur of voices from the drawing room grew louder, and George paused outside the door, gathering his courage.

"George, is that you?" His mother's voice called out. "Do come in, darling. We've been expecting you."

Taking a deep breath, George pushed open the door and stepped into the warmth of the drawing room. The fire crackled merrily in the hearth, casting a golden glow over the assembled family. His father, William Carter, sat in his favourite armchair, a tumbler of brandy in one hand and the evening newspaper forgotten in his lap. Margaret Carter perched on the settee, her embroidery set aside as she rose to greet her son. And there, by the window, stood Robert, George's older brother, his face etched with concern.

"My boy," William Carter boomed, rising to his feet. Come, sit. You have something to tell us, don't you?"

"I'm assuming that's why you asked me to come here, Father. And yes, I have some rather distressing news."

Margaret's brow furrowed as she guided George to a seat. "Whatever is the matter, dear? You look positively ill. You should be looking radiant after your engagement announcement? And how is Grace? She looked divine in the taffeta last night, don't you think?"

George clasped his hands together, willing them to stop trembling. "It's about Grace and the engagement."

William's face remained impassive whilst Robert stood by the window, and Margaret looked confused.

"I've called off the engagement."

A stunned silence fell over the room. Margaret gasped, her hand flying to her throat. Robert straightened, moving away from the window to stand by his brother.

William's face darkened like a storm cloud gathering on the horizon. "So, the rumour is true?" His voice was dangerously quiet.

George swallowed hard, forcing himself to meet his father's gaze. "I've ended my engagement to Grace Pembroke. I cannot, in good conscience, marry her."

"Cannot in good conscience?" William repeated, his voice rising. "What in God's name are you talking about, boy? The Pembrokes are one of the most respected families in Blackstone. This match was to secure our position in society, to ensure the future of the Carter name!"

"William, please," Margaret interjected, reaching out to place a calming hand on her husband's arm. "Let George explain. I'm sure he has a good reason for such a drastic decision."

George nodded gratefully to his mother before continuing. "I've discovered something terrible about the Pembroke family. They're involved with the resurrectionists."

"That's a serious accusation, George," Margaret said, her voice laced with concern.

"It's more than that," George pressed on, the words tumbling out now that he'd begun. "They're not just involved with the resurrectionists. They've been orchestrating the whole operation. The murders, the grave robberies, they all lead back to the Pembrokes."

Margaret sank back onto the settee, her face ashen. "Oh, George. Are you certain? This is monstrous."

William, however, remained unmoved. "And where, pray tell, did you come by this information? Some idle gossip at the fete, perhaps? Or maybe..." His eyes narrowed. "Maybe it was Miss Morgan who put these ideas in your head."

George felt a flash of anger at the insinuation. "I've seen evidence, letters in Grace's uncle's own hand detailing instructions to the gang."

"Letters?" Robert leaned forward, intrigued despite himself. "You've seen these letters yourself?"

George hesitated for a moment. "Well, no. Not personally. But Hetty—"

"Ah, there it is!" William exclaimed, slamming his tumbler down on the side table. "Miss Morgan again. I might have known she'd be at the root of this madness."

"Father, please," George implored. "This isn't about Hetty. It's about justice, about doing what's right. How can I marry into a family that's responsible for such atrocities?"

William began to pace the room, his agitation palpable. "Do you have any idea what you've done? The scandal this will cause? You've not only jeopardised your own future but the standing of our entire family!"

"William," Margaret interjected, her voice soft but firm. "Perhaps we should hear George out. If what he says is true..."

"If?" William scoffed. "My dear, surely you can see what's really going on here. Our son has allowed himself to be led astray by that Morgan girl. She's filled his head with these wild tales, all in an attempt to sabotage his engagement."

George stood abruptly, his hands clenched at his sides. "That's not fair, father. Hetty is not some scheming temptress. She's a woman of intelligence and integrity, and she—"

"She's the reason you're throwing away everything we've worked for!" William roared. "Don't think I haven't seen the way you look at her, George. This... this fabrication about the Pembrokes is nothing more than an excuse for you to pursue your infatuation!"

The accusation hung in the air, heavy and suffocating. George felt as though he'd been struck, the truth of his feelings for Hetty laid bare before his family. He opened his mouth to protest, but no words came.

It was Robert who broke the tense silence. "George," he said gently, "are your feelings for Miss Morgan influencing your judgement in this matter?"

George sank back into his chair, suddenly feeling very small under the weight of his family's scrutiny. "I... I won't deny that I care for Hetty," he admitted quietly. "But that doesn't change the facts about the Pembrokes. Even if Hetty weren't in the picture, I couldn't go through with the marriage knowing what I know now."

Margaret rose and crossed to her younger son, placing a comforting hand on his shoulder. "Oh, my darling boy. Love can indeed make fools of us all. But George, you must understand the gravity of what you're proposing. To break an engagement, to accuse the Pembrokes of such heinous crimes... it's not something to be done lightly."

"I know, Mother," George said, covering her hand with his own. "Believe me, I've agonised over this decision. But I cannot in good conscience bind myself to a family involved in such evil deeds."

William, who had been glowering by the fireplace, turned back to face his son. "And what of your conscience when our family is ruined by scandal? Have you given any thought to that?"

Robert shifted uncomfortably. "Father, please. I'm sure George has considered—"

"Has he?" William interrupted. "Has he truly? Or has he been too blinded by his infatuation with Hetty Morgan to see reason?"

George felt a surge of frustration. "This isn't about Hetty! Why can't you understand that? This is about doing what's right, about standing up against a grave injustice!"

"An injustice you have no proof of!" William countered. "Nothing but hearsay and the word of a woman who stands to benefit from the dissolution of your engagement!"

"William, that's quite enough," Margaret said firmly. "Regardless of his motivations, George is a grown man capable of making his own decisions."

"Decisions that affect us all," William muttered darkly.

A heavy silence fell over the room. George looked from face to face—his father's anger, his mother's concern, Robert's conflicted expression—and felt a wave of despair wash over him. He had hoped for understanding, for support, but instead found himself adrift in a sea of doubt and recrimination.

"Perhaps," Robert ventured after a moment, "we should all take some time to consider what George has told us. Can we verify these accusations against the Pembrokes without causing a public scandal?"

George ran a hand through his hair, his mind racing. "I... I'm not sure. The evidence Hetty found was in her father's ledger. He's been implicated as well, though she believes he's being framed."

William scoffed. "Of course she does. How convenient."

"Father, please," Robert said, shooting George a sympathetic look. "What if we were to approach this discreetly? Perhaps I could make some inquiries, see if there's any substance to these claims before we take any drastic action."

Margaret nodded eagerly. "Yes, that seems sensible. We mustn't be hasty in such a delicate matter."

George felt a glimmer of hope. "You'd do that, Robert? Thank you. I know it's a lot to ask, but—"

"It's the least I can do," Robert said with a small smile. "After all, what are brothers for if not to help navigate life's stormier waters?"

William, however, remained unconvinced. "And in the meantime? What of George's engagement? What of our standing in the community?"

"Perhaps," Margaret suggested gently, "we could say that George and Grace have decided to extend their courtship. That they wish to be absolutely certain before taking such a momentous step. It would buy us some time without raising suspicion."

George nodded slowly. "That... that could work. Grace knows the truth, of course, but she has as much reason as we do to avoid a public scandal."

William's shoulders sagged, the fight seeming to drain out of him. "Very well," he said wearily. "We'll proceed with caution. But George," he added, fixing his son with a stern gaze, "if these accusations prove false, if this has all been some flight of fancy..."

"They won't be," George said firmly. "I stake my reputation on it."

As the family dispersed, each lost in their own thoughts, George found himself alone by the window. The grounds of the Carter estate stretched out before him, bathed in moonlight. In the distance, he could just make out the lights of Blackstone, twinkling like stars fallen to earth.

His thoughts turned to Hetty, to the stolen moments they'd shared, to the future that now seemed tantalisingly within reach. But at what cost? The disapproval of his family weighed heavily upon him, as did the knowledge of the storm that was surely brewing in the Pembroke household.

A soft knock at the door roused George from his reverie. Robert entered, two glasses of brandy in hand. He offered one to George, who accepted it gratefully.

"You've stirred up quite the hornet's nest, little brother," Robert said, taking a sip of his drink.

George sighed. "I know. I never meant to cause such turmoil. I only wanted to do what was right."

Robert studied him for a long moment. "As long as you are making the right decision, I will stand by you."

George felt a flush creep up his neck. "Thank you, Robert. Hetty is remarkable. Brilliant, compassionate, unafraid to stand up for what she believes in. I've never met anyone like her."

"I see," Robert said, a knowing smile playing at the corners of his mouth. "And you're certain your feelings for her haven't clouded your judgement in this matter?"

George turned to face his brother fully. "I won't deny that I care for Hetty deeply. But Robert, could you marry anyone if you knew their family had been involved in matters such as these?"

Robert nodded slowly. "I believe you, George. And for what it's worth, I think you're doing the right thing. It won't be easy, mind you. Father will come around eventually, but it may take some time."

"And you?" George asked hesitantly. "What do you think of all this?"

Robert clapped a hand on George's shoulder. "I think my little brother has grown into a man of principle. And I couldn't be prouder."

George felt a lump form in his throat. "Thank you, Robert. That means more than you know."

As the two brothers stood in companionable silence, gazing out at the moonlit grounds, George felt a glimmer of hope. Little did he know that far across town, in the shadowy recesses of the Pembroke estate, plans were already being set in motion.

Chapter Thirty-Two

Hetty sat alone in the dimly lit kitchen, the remnants of the harvest fete's laughter still echoing in her mind. A candle flickered on the side table, casting long shadows that seemed to play out the day's events over and again on the walls. She twirled a curl of auburn hair around her finger, a habit she fell back on when deep in thought.

"Hetty?" George Carter stood at the threshold, his figure outlined by the setting sun streaming in from the open doorway.

"George!" Hetty rose quickly, smoothing out her skirts. Her heart thrummed with nervous energy. "I did not expect you."

"May I?" He gestured towards the chair opposite her, seeking permission to enter.

"Of course," she replied, motioning him to a chair. "Please sit."

George stepped inside, closing the door behind him. He took the offered seat while Hetty resumed her own, folding her hands in her lap to hide their trembling.

"I find myself quite elated to be here," he began, his eyes meeting hers with an intensity that belied his composed exterior. "But I am also apprehensive about what is to come."

"Elated?" Hetty echoed, a faint smile touching her lips despite the turmoil within.

"Indeed." George leaned forward, his brown eyes earnest. "Last night was illuminating. The connection between us—it has grown stronger, has it not?"

"It has," she admitted softly, the truth undeniable. "But we must tread carefully, George. Grace—her position in society, her authority, her expectations, they could ruin everything."

"Grace is a matter for another time," he interrupted gently. "For now, I am here for you, to discuss our future. And I am fully aware of the risks involved."

Hetty felt her resolve wavering under the weight of his gaze, the promise of a future she had scarcely allowed herself to dream of. Yet, Grace's image loomed in her thoughts, a reminder of the complexities they faced.

"Are we to be foolish then? Casting aside propriety for feelings that may very well lead to ruin?" Hetty asked, though her voice lacked conviction.

"Sometimes, Hetty," George said, reaching across to take her hand in his, "the most profound acts are those mistaken for folly by others. Our intentions are honest, our cause just."

"Perhaps," she whispered, allowing herself a moment to relish the warmth of his touch before withdrawing her hand. "But honesty does not shield one from consequence."

George stood and started to pace the room in front of the hearth, his hands clasped behind his back, casting long shadows on the faded Persian rug. Hetty watched him from the edge of the chair, her hands folded neatly in her lap, her mind racing with the gravity of their situation.

"George," she began, her voice steady despite the tempest within, "society will not look kindly on us now you have broken your engagement to Grace."

He stopped pacing and faced her, his brown eyes earnest. "I know. My family's name, my future in medicine—it could all be tarnished by scandal."

Hetty felt a pang of guilt, yet she knew that their feelings could not be bound by societal constraints alone. "And Grace," she added softly, "what of her reputation?"

"Grace is strong, resourceful," George said, though a crease of concern formed between his brows. "She will not be easily cast aside. She has her own ambitions, ones that do not necessarily require me by her side."

"Still," Hetty murmured, "to end an engagement is no small matter. It will set tongues wagging, and in such dangerous times." Her words trailed off as a shiver ran down her spine.

George knelt beside her, taking her hand once more, his touch a balm to her fraying nerves. "Hetty, I cannot pretend to understand all the dangers your father faces, but I do know this: nothing is more perilous than living a life devoid of truth."

She met his gaze, her blue eyes reflecting a tumult of emotions. "Truth is a luxury we may not afford. I fear for my father every day, and these murders," she said, biting her lip. "The constabulary is at a loss, and with each passing day, the whispers grow louder, the suspicions darker."

"Your father is a good man, caught in an unfortunate trade," George assured her. "We must find a way to clear his name, to lift this shadow from over your house."

"Can we?" Hetty asked, hope mingling with doubt. "Or are we merely inviting further misfortune upon ourselves?"

"Perhaps," he conceded, squeezing her hand gently. "But I would rather face misfortune with you than endure a hollow existence without you."

The fire's glow waned to a subtle flicker, casting long shadows across the room as George released Hetty's hand and stood with a resolute air. "I've watched you carry this burden alone for far too long, Hetty. Your father's honour, your family's peace, they are not yours to shoulder without aid."

Hetty looked up at him, her eyes catching the firelight. "George, do you understand what you're saying? This isn't simply about breaking an engagement—this is about delving into perilous waters. The outcome could be dire."

"Then let the outcome be ours to face, together," he said. "I cannot in good conscience stand by while injustice festers in the heart of the town. Nor can I bear the thought of your spirit, so bright and unyielding, dimmed by these tragedies."

"Your family...," she began, but George shook his head.

"I think they will come round. Maybe not fully, and you may never be accepted. But my allegiance lies with the truth—and with you."

"Even if it leads us into danger?" Hetty's voice was steady, but her hands betrayed her as they twisted the fabric of her skirt.

"Especially then." He knelt before her, taking her hands in his.

"Come, I have something to show you," Hetty said. She suddenly stood up and led George to her father's study, the nerve centre of his clandestine operation. She clicked the door shut behind them with a quiet certainty that belied the trembling in her fingers. The room was steeped in the musty scent of old paper and leather—a testament to her father's meticulous record-keeping.

"Here," she said, placing the notes on the polished mahogany desk. "This is the account of every transaction he's made. But there's more to it than numbers."

"Go on," George urged, leaning closer.

"Father kept detailed notes beside each entry. Dates, names—even peculiarities about the deceased." Hetty flipped through the pages, her eyes scanning quickly until they paused, widening slightly. "Look here," she gestured toward an entry marked with a small cross.

George peered down at the cursive script. *'Florence Henry, age thirty-two, succumbed to consumption.'* "Why the cross?"

"Every marked entry—each one represents someone who died under questionable circumstances." Hetty's voice dropped to a whisper, heavy with implication.

"Good heavens," George murmured, his brow furrowed in thought. "You think these deaths may be linked to the bodysnatchers?"

"It's possible," she nodded. "If we can prove a connection to the murders in the town, we can expose the true extent of this vile trade."

"Your father was a brave man to keep such records," George said, admiration softening his voice.

"Brave, but not foolish," Hetty corrected. "He never kept the ledger in one piece. He would hide portions of it, in case his papers were ever found. But I also believe that letters have been planted in his ledgers."

George acknowledged with a nod.

"Which brings me to my next point." Hetty hesitated, her gaze locked with his. "We cannot do this alone. We need more allies."

"Frederick and Beatrice," George said almost at once.

"Yes. They're clever, resourceful, and could be invaluable. They are keen to help and it's important that they get justice for Archibald, we must help them do that. They firmly believe Archibald was murdered."

"Then we must continue to allow them to help, they are both keen so let's collaborate with them. We shall speak to them both."

"Of course," Hetty nodded. "But we must be careful not to draw undue attention to our efforts."

"Discretion will be our watchword," he assured her.

"Thank you, George," she said, her blue eyes reflecting a mix of gratitude and resolve. "With your help, we might just bring light to these shadows."

"Then let's waste no more time," he declared, his hand resting briefly on her shoulder before he turned towards the door. "We have much to do."

"George..." Hetty had moved to the window to draw the curtain, a muffled cacophony from the cobblestone street below snagged her attention. She paused, her fingertips grazing the heavy fabric. "George, listen," she whispered urgently.

He joined her at the window, his presence a reassuring solidity in the dim room. They peered through a sliver of space between the curtains, careful to remain unseen.

Two shadowy figures stood beneath the flickering glow of a gas lamp, their voices a conspiratorial hiss carried upward on the evening breeze.

"Are they speaking of...?" Hetty's voice trailed off as she strained to make out the words.

"Shh, let's not jump to conclusions," George cautioned, his brow furrowed as he listened intently.

"Can't be taking no risks," one figure muttered, a gruff timbre lacing his speech.

"Right, with the body snatchers and all, we've got enough troubles," the other replied, a nervous laugh punctuating his statement.

Hetty felt a chill despite the closeness of the room. The conversation was veering too close to the subject of their own clandestine investigations.

"Bodysnatchers?" George echoed under his breath, his face grave. "It seems our fears are not unfounded." George turned away from the window, his expression contemplative. "My family," he began hesitantly, "they are not taking kindly to this investigation of ours. I'm wondering whether it is my father who is having us followed?"

"Will they not understand? We're trying to do what's right," she said, her voice laced with concern.

"Understand? Perhaps. Approve? That's another matter entirely." He sighed, his aristocratic upbringing warring with his conscience. "The Carters have their reputation to consider. Scandal is not something we entertain lightly."

"Nor do we Morgans," Hetty countered softly, "but I fear that ship has long since sailed for both our families."

"True," he conceded, a rueful smile touching his lips.

"Perhaps there are connections we've yet to see." George's eyes shone with analytical precision. "And we should speak with those who knew the victims, discreetly. Gather stories, testimonies."

"Discreetly being the operative word," Hetty mused.

"Then let us be cautious in whom we trust," George interjected. He stopped his pacing and stood before her, his gaze earnest. "Hetty, we must also consider how this—we—will appear to the outside world.

Which is why," George took a step closer, his voice barely above a whisper, "we must guard our hearts in public." His hand reached out, hovering just shy of touching hers before he drew back. "No matter how genuine the feelings that lie beneath."

"Hide our affection as though it were part of the investigation itself," Hetty added, her own hand aching to bridge the gap between them. "A secret kept behind closed doors."

"Exactly so," he confirmed, the corner of his mouth lifting in a wistful smile. But remember, Hetty," George said, his brown eyes locking with hers, "it's merely a masquerade. One day, we won't have to hide."

"One day," she whispered.

Chapter Thirty-Three

Hetty and her companions were preparing for their nocturnal expedition to the docks. The moon hung low over the Thames as the four made their way through the winding alleys, the sound of lapping water and creaking wood growing louder as they approached their destination.

"There," Frederick whispered, pointing to a dilapidated structure looming in the darkness. "That must be the warehouse."

"George! You made it, I was getting rather worried about you."

"I'm sorry I'm late, I had trouble with my father," he whispered.

"Oh, George, I'm sorry. Sorry for all the trouble I have caused."

"Nonsense, Hetty. I want a conclusion to the resurrectionists as much as you do. And I won't adhere to my father's wishes when it involves marrying a woman connected to the torrid gang," George smiled meekly at Hetty under the moonlight. "Anyway, let's move on, we have work to do."

"I have news too. I have concerns about my father. I haven't seen him since I returned home to visit him, I'm getting worried."

George took Hetty's hand in his. "We will find him. First, let's get this over with."

They crept closer, hearts pounding in their chests. As they neared, a flicker of movement caught Hetty's eye. "Look," she hissed, gesturing to a figure slipping out from behind the building's weathered doors.

The moonlight caught the person's face for just a moment, but it was enough. Hetty's blood ran cold as she recognised the delicate features of Grace Pembroke.

"What in God's name is she doing here?" Frederick muttered, voicing the question on all their minds.

Before they could decide on a course of action, a commotion from within the warehouse drew their attention. The doors burst open, and several men emerged, pushing a cart laden with an ominous, shrouded shape.

"We need to get closer," Hetty insisted, already moving forward despite Frederick's attempt to hold her back.

As they edged nearer, hidden in the shadows of stacked crates, snippets of conversation drifted to their ears.

"...another successful extraction. The doctors will be pleased."

"Aye, but we must be more careful. There's talk in town, suspicions rising."

"Let them talk. We have protection in high places."

Hetty's eyes widened as she recognised one of the voices—it belonged to Grace's uncle.

Suddenly, a hand clamped down on Hetty's shoulder. She whirled, a scream rising in her throat, only to find herself face to face with Robert Carter.

"What are you doing here?" George hissed, surprise and confusion evident in his voice.

"Following a hunch," Robert replied grimly. "And it seems I was right to be concerned. You shouldn't be here—none of you should. It's not safe."

"We can't just walk away," Hetty argued, her voice low but intense. "We've seen too much."

A shout from the direction of the warehouse cut their debate short. "Oi! Who's there?"

"Run!" Robert commanded, pushing them towards the maze of alleyways.

They fled into the night; the sound of pursuit close behind. Hetty's heart raced as they navigated the narrow passages, the echo of footsteps spurring them on.

Finally, after what seemed an eternity, they emerged onto a quiet street, gasping for breath. The sounds of their pursuers had faded, lost in the warren of the docklands.

"Is everyone alright?" George asked, his eyes scanning the group.

Nods and murmured affirmations followed, the reality of what they had witnessed settling over them like a heavy shroud.

"We need to regroup," Hetty said, her mind already racing with the implications of what they'd seen. "We'll decide our next move tomorrow."

George grabbed Hetty's elbow before she walked away. His touch was gentle, but his eyes held a fierce determination. "Hetty, please be careful. Nowhere is safe."

Hetty blinked slowly, a small smile forming on her lips. "I will, I promise."

George's grip tightened slightly, his voice dropping to a near whisper. "You know where I am if you need me... if you need to call. My father may not approve, but he will have to understand. I want to be there for you if danger strikes."

Hetty's eyes widened in surprise. "But George, your father—"

"My father will have to understand," George reiterated, his jaw set with resolve. "This is bigger than his disappointment or society's expectations. You're more important to me than any of that."

A faint blush coloured Hetty's cheeks. "George, I—"

"I know it's not ideal," he continued, his eyes never leaving hers. "The thought of you calling at my parents' house might set tongues wagging. But your safety, your well-being... they mean more to me than airs and graces. More than my father's approval or any arranged marriage."

Hetty's hand found his, squeezing it gently. "Thank you, George. Your support means everything to me."

Little did Hetty know that across town, in the shadowed confines of his study, William Carter was penning a letter that would set in motion events that would test their resolve to its very limits. The stakes were higher than any of them could ever imagine.

Chapter Thirty-Four

Hetty's steps faltered. The front door stood slightly ajar, a silent sentinel to some unknown drama. With trembling hands, she pushed it open, her eyes widening at the scene before her.

The entryway was in disarray, a side table overturned, and her father's favourite walking stick lay broken on the floor. Hetty's breath caught in her throat as she moved further into the house, calling out, "Father? Father, are you here?"

Only silence answered her pleas. In Thomas's study, papers were strewn about, drawers pulled from the desk and emptied. It was clear someone had been searching for something—or someone.

She crept upstairs, frightened to disturb any unwarranted thief or worse, kidnapper. Hetty pushed open her father's bedroom door with one finger. The door creaked open, breaking the silence in the house. Her father's bed was empty, the sheets cold and undisturbed. It wasn't like Thomas Morgan to leave without a word, especially given the precarious nature of their current situation.

Hetty walked over to her father's chair by his bed, sank into it, and sighed deeply, her mind reeling. She didn't shout or scream, hammer at the window, or run out of the house and down the street. Because what good would it do? She knew, with a certainty that chilled her to her core, that Thomas Morgan had not left of his own accord. He had been taken, and she had little doubt as to why. As she stared at the wall in front of her, she gritted her teeth and decided she would get him back no matter what.

A soft knock at the front door startled her from her thoughts. Hetty stood up and walked downstairs. She tentatively opened the door, wondering who it might be as no visitors were planned.

George Carter stood in the doorway.

"George? Oh, George!" She fell into his arms as he caught her and pulled her into his chest. He wrapped his arms around her and stroked her hair. "Hetty, shh, what is it, my love?"

"Please, come in, I don't want anyone to see us like this and make matters worse."

Hetty stepped inside and George followed. George closed the door behind him and watched Hetty walk to the front room and sit down. She beckoned him to sit next to her.

"My father has gone."

"Gone? Gone where?" He said quizzically.

"He's been taken. His bed is made, and there is no sign of him. I was about to enter his workshop when you arrived."

"Hetty, this is terrible, you don't think it's the resurrectionists, do you?"

Hetty looked at George and raised her eyebrows. "There is no other answer, George. With everything that has happened, I knew his life would be in danger. Come," she said, leading the way to her father's workshop.

George's expression grew grave as he surveyed the chaos around them. Ledgers were strewn across workbenches, jars had been smashed, and sheets that covered dead bodies, torn to shreds.

"We'll find him, Hetty. I swear it."

Chapter Thirty-Five

As the night wore on, Hetty and George planned their return to the warehouse by the docks in darkness. They hoped to find some clue as to Thomas' whereabouts.

They made their way through the shadowy streets, every sense alert for danger.

A derelict building with smashed windows loomed before them. With practised stealth, they slipped inside, the musty air thick with the scent of damp wood and something less identifiable—something that spoke of secrets best left buried.

"Look here," George whispered, gesturing to a locked door. He turned side on to the door and rushed towards it using his force to open it.

The door eventually gave way and Hetty walked past George and stepped inside.

"George, look," she said, running her fingers over a dusty ledger. "These are some of Blackstone's most prominent citizens," she breathed. "Magistrates, doctors, even your father's name is here."

George's face paled in the dim light. "It can't be. There must be some mistake."

But even as he spoke, nothing could deny the words and numbers on the yellowing pages. The conspiracy ran deeper than they had ever imagined, reaching into the very heart of the town's most elite of residents.

Suddenly, the sound of footsteps got closer. Hastily, they retreated into the shadows and crouched down behind the desk. They held their breath as two figures entered the warehouse.

"The Morgan girl is becoming a problem," a gravelly voice said. "She's asking too many questions, digging too deep."

"Then perhaps it's time we sent her a message she can't ignore," replied a second voice, chillingly familiar. It was Grace Pembroke's uncle, his cultured tones at odds with the menace in his words.

Hetty and George exchanged a glance, their hearts pounding.

Chapter Thirty-Six

When the coast was clear, they slipped away into the night, their minds racing with the implications of what they'd overheard.

Once they were a safe distance from the warehouse, George pulled Hetty into a shadowy alcove, his voice barely above a whisper. "Hetty, did you hear that? They're targeting you specifically now."

Hetty nodded, her face pale in the dim moonlight. "I heard. But George, we can't stop now. We're so close to uncovering the truth."

"Close to the truth, and close to mortal danger," George hissed, his grip on Hetty's arm tightening. "That was Grace's uncle in there. Do you understand what that means? This conspiracy reaches higher than we ever imagined."

Hetty's eyes flashed with determination. "All the more reason to press on. We can't let them continue these horrible deeds, George. We can't!"

George ran a hand through his hair, frustration evident in every line of his body. "I know, Hetty. Believe me, I know. But they're talking about sending you a message. In their world, that will mean violence."

"Let them try," Hetty whispered fiercely. "I won't be cowed by threats. My father is missing, George. He could be..." She couldn't finish the sentence, her voice catching.

George's expression softened. He cupped Hetty's face gently, his thumb brushing away a tear she hadn't realised had fallen. "We'll find him, Hetty. I promise you that. But no more late-night excursions to derelict buildings. It's too dangerous."

Hetty leaned into his touch, drawing strength from his presence. "What do you suggest then? We can't just sit idle while they continue their ghastly work."

"We gather our allies, consolidate what we know, and take the concrete evidence to the authorities."

"The authorities?" Hetty scoffed quietly. "How do we know they're not involved as well? Your father's name was on that list, George. Who's to say the police aren't equally complicit?"

George's jaw clenched at the mention of his father. "We have to believe there are still good people in positions of power. We just need to find them."

Hetty nodded slowly, her mind working furiously. "We need to be careful whom we trust. Tonight proved that the enemy could be anyone, even those closest to us."

"Agreed," George whispered. He glanced around nervously, suddenly aware of how exposed they were, even in the shadowy alcove. "We should move. It's not safe to linger."

As they prepared to step back onto the street, Hetty caught George's arm. "George, I... I'm afraid," she admitted, her voice barely audible. "Not for myself, but for my father, for you, for all of us."

"I know, Hetty, I know," George said, stroking her hair.

Little did they know that their whispered conversation had not gone entirely unheard. In the shadows across the street, a figure melted away into the night.

Chapter Thirty-Seven

◈

The following days brought a whirlwind of activity and mounting tension. Robert sought out George, pulling him aside after another strained family dinner. The brothers retreated to the library, away from their father's disapproving glares.

"George," Robert began, his voice low and concerned, "I want you to know that I support you in this. But father's patience is wearing thin."

George's jaw clenched. "I can't stop now, Robert. We're close to uncovering the truth. Father's name was on that list—don't you want to know why?"

"Of course I do," Robert replied, placing a reassuring hand on his brother's shoulder. "And I'm with you. But we need to be smart about this. Father may be angry, but he's more concerned about gossip than he is about your choices."

George nodded, understanding dawning in his eyes. "That's why he hasn't thrown me out, isn't it? He'd rather have me here under his roof than risk the scandal of his son *'living in sin'* or on the streets."

"Exactly," Robert confirmed. "He might not approve of your investigation or your... feelings for Miss Morgan, but he'll tolerate it to keep up appearances. Use that to your advantage, George. Stay here where it's safe, where we can protect you."

"And where I can protect Hetty if need be," George added softly.

Robert's expression grew serious. "Just be careful, brother. We're dealing with powerful people."

As the brothers strategised, across town Grace Pembroke was holding court in the town's most fashionable tea room. Her voice dripped with barely concealed venom as she addressed her rapt audience.

"It's such a shame about poor Hetty Morgan," she sighed. "To think, a young woman of her standing, sneaking about at all hours with a man. And not just any man, it's positively scandalous."

The other ladies tittered behind their fans, their eyes alight with the thrill of gossip. Grace's campaign of whispers and innuendo was gaining momentum, slowly but surely tarnishing Hetty's reputation.

Beatrice, overhearing the conversation from a nearby table, felt her blood boil. She longed to confront Grace, to defend Hetty's honour, but she knew such an outburst would only add fuel to the fire. Instead, she quietly excused herself, her mind working furiously.

Later that evening, Beatrice burst into Hetty's home, her face flushed with excitement. "I've found something," she announced to the assembled group. "Another link between the Pembrokes and those unsolved murders from last year."

As Beatrice laid out her discovery—financial records showing large sums transferred to known criminals on the dates of the murders—the gravity of their situation became even clearer.

"This goes beyond mere bodysnatching," Frederick mused, his brow furrowed. "It's as if the entire upper echelon of Blackstone is engaged in some grand, ghastly experiment."

Hetty nodded, her mind racing. "The Medical Society," she said suddenly. "Don't you see? It's the perfect cover. Respected doctors with access to the latest research, wealthy patrons to fund their work, and a steady supply of subjects."

The room fell silent as the implications sank in.

Chapter Thirty-Eight

⁘

The next morning found George once again in his father's study, facing down William Carter's wrath.

"This madness ends now, George," William thundered. "I've indulged in your little detective game long enough. You will cease this investigation immediately, or so help me ..."

George stood his ground, his voice steady. "I can't do that, Father. We're close to uncovering the truth. And your name was on a list we found. A list of those involved with the resurrectionists. Tell me it isn't true."

William's face paled, then flushed with anger. "You dare accuse me? Your own father? Get out of my sight. You're no son of mine."

As George turned to leave, his mother's voice stopped him. "George, please," Margaret Carter pleaded. "Think of what you're throwing away. Your family, your future. Is it worth it?"

George's heart ached at the pain in his mother's voice, but his resolve didn't waver. "It's not just about Hetty, Mother. It's about doing what's right. I'm sorry, but I can't turn back now."

As night fell over the town, Hetty, George, Frederick, and Beatrice gathered to take stock of their situation. The evidence of corruption, the threats against Thomas Morgan, his disappearance, the ledgers, the overheard conversations—it all painted a picture of a conspiracy far larger and more insidious than they had ever imagined.

"We're dealing with more than just criminals," Hetty said, her voice steady despite the fear that gnawed at her. "This is the town's elite, using their power and influence to protect a trade in death and suffering."

George nodded grimly. "And they'll stop at nothing to keep their secrets buried."

As they talked late into the night, little did they know that across town, in a dimly lit room, a group of Blackstone's most influential citizens was gathering. Among them were faces that would have shocked Hetty and her friends—pillars of the community, men of science and law, all united in a dark purpose.

As they spoke in hushed tones of progress and necessary sacrifices, of grand visions and the greater good, at the centre of it all, a figure stepped from the shadows—a man whose identity would shake the very foundations of everything Hetty and George thought they knew.

Chapter Thirty-Nine

The morning mist clung to the cobblestones, shrouding the town in an ethereal haze. George Carter walked briskly through the streets, his mind churning with the revelations of the previous night. The weight of the conspiracy they had uncovered pressed heavily upon him, each step feeling like a march towards an uncertain fate.

As he rounded the corner onto Willow Street, a familiar figure emerged from the fog. Grace Pembroke stood before him, her golden curls perfectly coiffed despite the early hour. George's steps faltered, his body tensing involuntarily.

THE DAUGHTER'S ENDURING LOVE 185

"George," Grace called, her voice honey sweet. "Might I have a word?"

Reluctantly, George approached. "Grace, I don't think—"

"Please," she interrupted, her eyes wide and imploring. "I know things have been... difficult between us. But I want you to know that I forgive you."

George blinked, taken aback. "Forgive me?"

Grace nodded earnestly. "For your indiscretions with Miss Morgan. I understand, truly. You were led astray, but it's not too late to make things right."

"Make things right?" George repeated, a hint of steel entering his voice.

"Yes, darling," Grace continued, seemingly oblivious to his tone. "If you'll only cease this foolish investigation, we can put this all behind us. We can be together, as we were always meant to be."

For a moment, George was tempted. The promise of an easy return to his old life, to the comfort and security he had known, was alluring. But then he thought of Hetty, of the truths they had uncovered, of the lives at stake.

"I'm sorry, Grace," he said finally, his voice firm. "But I can't do that. What we've discovered goes beyond you and me. I won't turn a blind eye to the suffering of others, not even for the sake of our engagement."

Grace's expression hardened, the mask of sweetness slipping. "You're making a grave mistake, George. You have no idea of the forces you're up against."

"Perhaps not," George replied. "But I know which side I'm on." With that, he turned and walked away, leaving Grace staring after him, her face a mixture of anger and something that might have been fear.

Across town, Robert Carter sat in his study, poring over a stack of documents. His eyes widened as he connected names, dates, and transactions. It was circumstantial, yes, but the pattern was clear. The Pembrokes, the Rutherfords, even the Carters themselves—all had financial ties to businesses that could easily serve as fronts for the resurrectionist trade.

A knock at the door startled him from his thoughts. "Come in," he called, hastily covering the papers.

George entered, his face drawn with worry. "Robert, I need your help. Things are escalating, and I fear we're running out of time."

Robert hesitated, torn between his loyalty to his family and his growing certainty that George was onto something sinister. Finally, he made his decision. "Alright, George. Tell me everything."

Chapter Forty

Hetty Morgan made her way to the local market, her mind preoccupied with thoughts of her missing father. She was so lost in her worries that she didn't notice George approaching until he was right beside her.

"Hetty," he said softly, touching her arm. "Any word?"

She shook her head, blinking back tears. "Nothing. It's as if he's vanished into thin air."

George pulled her into a comforting embrace, propriety be damned. Neither of them noticed Grace Pembroke watching from across the square, her eyes narrowing at the intimate display.

"Well, well," Grace murmured to her companion. "It seems Miss Morgan's fall from grace is even more complete than we thought."

The whispers spread through the market like wildfire, fuelled by Grace's carefully crafted insinuations. By nightfall, Hetty's reputation would be in tatters.

Meanwhile, Beatrice had been conducting her own investigation. She sat now in the study of her modest home, spreading out a series of letters and documents before Frederick which Robert had passed on to them.

"Look here," she said, pointing to a series of names. "The Pembrokes, the Rutherfords, the Carters—they're all connected through this medical society. And look at the dates of these meetings. They coincide perfectly with the reported disappearances and grave robberies."

Frederick frowned, a crease of worry deepening between his brows. "Ma, we should leave this to the proper authorities."

Beatrice's eyes flashed with indignation. "The proper authorities? Frederick, we can't trust anyone outside our circle."

"And what if our meddling puts Hetty in even greater danger?" Frederick countered, his voice rising. "Have you thought of that?"

Their argument was interrupted by a commotion outside. They rushed to the window to see a figure stumbling down the street—Thomas Morgan, looking dishevelled and disoriented.

Hetty, who had been on her way to meet Beatrice, saw her father and ran to him. "Father!" she cried, embracing him. But as she pulled back, she noticed something off in his gaze. His eyes were unfocused, and when he spoke, his words were slurred and disjointed.

"Hetty," he mumbled. "People are not what they seem. The Society... we have to stop them."

Before Hetty could question him further, Thomas's eyes rolled back, and he collapsed in her arms.

Chapter Forty-One

~~~~~~~~~~

As Thomas recuperated under Beatrice's care, the group made a decision. They would infiltrate the meeting of The Medical Society to be held that evening, gathering the evidence they needed to expose the truth once and for all.

"Remember," George whispered as they huddled together in the dim light of Beatrice's parlour, "we're not just doing this for ourselves. The fate of Blackstone itself hangs in the balance."

Hetty nodded, her face pale but determined. "Whatever happens in there, we must not lose sight of our purpose. We're the only ones who can stop this madness."

Under cover of darkness, they made their way to the imposing mansion where the Society met. The structure loomed before them, its windows glowing with an eerie light that seemed to mock their clandestine approach. Hetty and George exchanged a final, meaningful glance before slipping inside through a servant's entrance, while Frederick and Beatrice took up their positions outside.

The worn stone steps creaked beneath their feet as Hetty and George ascended, every sound amplified in the silence of the night. Hetty's heart pounded so loudly she feared it might give them away. As they neared the study, voices drifted through the heavy oak door, sending a chill down their spines.

With trembling hands, George eased the door open just a crack, allowing them to peer into the room beyond. The scene that greeted them in the grand study was like something out of a nightmare. Blackstone's most respected citizens gathered around a table, their faces cast in shadow by the flickering gaslight. The air was thick with cigar smoke and the underlying scent of something metallic and unpleasant.

"The morgue at St. Bartholomew's has been most cooperative," one man was saying, his voice dripping with smug satisfaction. "But we need fresher subjects for the more delicate experiments."

Hetty recognised the speaker as Dr Whitaker, a man her father had once spoken of with great respect. Now, his words turned her stomach.

"Perhaps it's time we expanded our operations," another suggested, leaning forward into the light. Hetty had to stifle a gasp as she recognised Judge Harrow, his usually stern face alive with a terrible eagerness. "The lower classes won't be missed, after all."

A murmur of agreement rippled through the assembled men. Hetty felt bile rise in her throat, but she forced herself to remain still, recording every word in her memory. George's hand found hers in the darkness, a silent reminder that she wasn't alone in this horror.

As they listened, the full scope of the conspiracy unfolded before them. It wasn't just about providing bodies for medical research—there were experiments, dark and twisted things that pushed the boundaries of science and morality.

"Gentlemen," a new voice spoke, silky smooth and terrifyingly familiar. Grace's uncle, Lord Pembroke, rose from his seat at the head of the table. "Let us not forget the greater purpose of our work. With each subject, each experiment, we push the boundaries of human knowledge. We stand on the cusp of discoveries that will revolutionise medicine, extend life itself!"

'At what cost?' Hetty thought, her mind reeling. She felt George tense beside her, his grip on her hand tightening.

Lord Pembroke continued, his voice rising with fervour. "The latest batch of subjects has yielded promising results. The reanimation process is showing signs of success."

A collective intake of breath swept through the room. Hetty's blood ran cold. Reanimation? Surely, they couldn't mean...

"We've managed to restore basic motor functions in Specimen 17," a reedy voice piped up. Hetty recognised Dr Simmons, the town's most renowned surgeon. "Heartbeat sustained for nearly three minutes post-revival."

"Excellent," Lord Pembroke nodded approvingly. "And the cognitive functions?"

Dr Simmons hesitated. "Still rudimentary. But with more fresh specimens, we could—"

"You'll have them," Judge Harrow interrupted. "I'll ensure any inconvenient inquiries are misdirected. The constabulary knows better than to dig too deeply."

Hetty's mind was spinning. The corruption ran deeper than they could have ever imagined. These men, pillars of the community, were playing God with people's lives, with death itself.

"What of the Morgan girl?" Dr Whitaker asked suddenly, causing Hetty's heart to nearly stop. "She and that Carter boy have been asking questions. Dangerous questions."

Lord Pembroke's face hardened. "They will be dealt with. Perhaps they might even contribute to our research, should the need arise."

Hetty bit back a cry of horror, George's arm around her waist the only thing keeping her from collapsing. They had to get out, had to warn the others.

As if in answer to her silent plea, a commotion erupted outside. A voice, raised in alarm, cut through the night air. "Oi! What do you think you're doing? This is private property!"

The men in the study jumped to their feet, papers scattering as they rushed to conceal their work. Hetty and George seized the moment of chaos to slip away, their hearts pounding as they fled down the servant's stairs.

They burst out into the cool night air, gasping. Frederick and Beatrice were there, hiding in the shadows, concern etched on their faces.

"We have to go, now," George panted. "They know we're onto them. It's worse than we thought, so much worse."

As they hurried through the darkened streets of Blackstone, Hetty's mind raced. The enormity of what they had uncovered threatened to overwhelm her. These men, these monsters masquerading as pillars of society, were not just grave robbers or body snatchers. They were tampering with the very essence of life and death, all in the name of progress.

"We need to tell someone," Beatrice whispered as they rounded a corner. "The authorities, the newspapers—someone must listen!"

"And who would believe us?" Frederick countered, his voice tight with fear. "We're up against the most powerful men in Blackstone. They control everything—the courts, the police, even the press."

"Then we'll make them believe," Hetty said, her voice steadier than she felt. "We have names now, details. We just need to show what we have."

George nodded grimly. "Whatever it takes, we'll expose them, we have to."

As they disappeared into the shadows, the weight of their discovery pressed down upon them. They were no longer just fighting to clear Thomas Morgan's name or to right a local wrong. They were standing against a darkness that threatened to consume their entire world.

Chapter Forty-Two

The morning dawned grey and foreboding over the smokey town, as if the very sky sensed the turmoil about to unfold. Hetty Morgan stood before the town hall, her heart pounding so fiercely she feared it might burst from her chest. Beside her, George Carter's presence was a steadying force, his hand finding hers in a brief, reassuring squeeze.

"Are you ready?" he whispered, his eyes searching her face.

Hetty took a deep breath, steeling herself. "As ready as I'll ever be. There's no turning back now."

With a nod to Frederick, who stood nearby clutching a stack of documents, they ascended the steps. The town square was already filling with curious onlookers, drawn by the hastily posted notices promising a revelation of utmost importance to every citizen of Blackstone.

As Hetty stepped up to the podium, a hush fell over the crowd. She could feel the weight of every eye upon her, could sense the mixture of curiosity and scepticism that rippled through the assembled townspeople. For a moment, her courage faltered. Then she caught sight of Beatrice's encouraging smile in the front row, and her resolve hardened.

"People of Blackstone," Hetty began, her voice ringing out clear and strong. "I stand before you today to unveil a truth that has long been hidden, a darkness that has festered in the very heart of our town."

As Hetty spoke, laying out the evidence they had gathered, the crowd's mood shifted palpably. Gasps of shock gave way to murmurs of disbelief, then to cries of outrage. She detailed the resurrectionist ring, the involvement of prominent citizens, the grisly experiments conducted in the name of science.

George stepped forward, adding his testimony to Hetty's. He named names—respected doctors, judges, even his own father—his voice never wavering despite the personal cost of his words.

From the corner of her eye, Hetty saw William Carter push through the crowd, his face a mask of fury. "Lies!" he bellowed, pointing an accusing finger at his son. "Vicious slander from a deranged boy and a pauper woman! It's all lies!"

George turned to face his father, his expression a mixture of sadness and determination. "Every word is true, Father. You stand there before me in denial, and you know it."

Henry's face contorted with rage. "You are no son of mine," he spat. "You're cut off, do you hear me? Disowned! You'll not see a penny of the Carter fortune!"

A shocked murmur ran through the crowd. George stood tall, even as Hetty saw the pain flash in his eyes. "So be it," he said quietly. "I choose truth over fortune, conscience over family name."

As William stormed away, Hetty felt a surge of admiration for George's courage. But there was no time to dwell on it. The revelations continued, each new detail sending fresh shockwaves through the assembled citizens of Blackstone.

Frederick stepped forward, distributing copies of key documents to members of the press who had gathered. Hetty caught sight of Grace Pembroke near the back of the crowd, her face pale with shock and growing fear.

As the full scope of the conspiracy unfolded, the mood of the crowd turned ugly. Angry shouts were directed at the Pembroke estate, calls for justice and retribution filling the air.

Suddenly, a commotion near the edge of the square drew everyone's attention. Thomas Morgan, looking haggard and haunted, pushed his way through the crowd.

"Father!" Hetty cried, rushing to his side.

Thomas gripped the podium, his knuckles white. "I must speak," he rasped. "I must... confess."

With halting words, Thomas revealed the extent of his involvement. He spoke of blackmail, of threats against Hetty's life that had forced his compliance. He detailed the bookkeeping he had done for the resurrectionist ring, the constant fear that had become his companion.

"I am not blameless," he concluded, his voice breaking. "I should have been stronger, should have resisted. But I beg you to understand—I acted out of love, out of fear for my daughter's life."

Hetty embraced her father, tears streaming down her face. The crowd's anger seemed to soften somewhat at this display of raw emotion, the complex reality of the situation sinking in.

As the meeting dispersed, the citizens of Blackstone left in a daze, struggling to come to terms with the horrifying truths that had been revealed. Hetty, George, and their allies huddled together, aware that they had set in motion events that would change their town forever.

In the days that followed, Blackstone was a town transformed. The initial shock gave way to a simmering anger, a demand for justice that could not be ignored. The police, under intense public pressure, were forced to launch a formal investigation.

Hetty and George found themselves at the centre of a maelstrom. Praised by some as heroes, vilified by others as troublemakers, they faced a new reality of whispers and pointed stares wherever they went.

"It's harder than I expected," Hetty confided to George one evening as they walked through the park, acutely aware of the eyes following them. "I knew there would be consequences, but this..."

George took her hand, his touch a comfort in the midst of the turmoil. "We knew it wouldn't be easy. But we did the right thing, Hetty. We have to hold onto that."

Their conversation was cut short by a commotion outside. Grace Pembroke stood in the street, surrounded by a group of townsfolk, her voice shrill with desperation.

"Don't be fooled by their lies!" she cried. "Hetty Morgan is nothing but a jealous, spiteful girl! She's fabricated this entire story to ruin my family, to steal George away from me!"

But Grace's words fell on deaf ears. The tide of public opinion had turned decisively against the Pembrokes. Her desperate attempts to discredit Hetty only served to make her appear more guilty in the eyes of the townspeople.

THE DAUGHTER'S ENDURING LOVE

As Grace was ushered away by concerned friends, Hetty felt a pang of pity beneath her anger. The woman she once admired for her strength was now a pathetic figure, clinging to the remnants of a life that was crumbling around her.

That evening, as Hetty and George pored over the mounting evidence in her father's study, a brick came crashing through the window. Attached was a note: "Stop now, or the next one won't miss."

George pulled Hetty close, his arms protective around her. "We knew they'd fight back," he murmured into her hair. "But I won't let them hurt you. We're in this together, remember?"

Hetty nodded, drawing strength from his presence. But as she looked at the shattered glass strewn across the floor, she couldn't shake the feeling that this was only the beginning of their troubles.

The next day brought fresh shocks. The local newspaper ran a front-page exposé on the Medical Society, revealing the true nature of their experiments. The story spoke of attempts to reanimate the dead, of cruel tests conducted on unwilling subjects, of a quest for immortality that had led brilliant minds down a dark and twisted path.

Blackstone reeled from the revelations. Citizens who had once respected and admired the town's leading figures now looked at them with fear and disgust. The streets buzzed with fearful whispers and wild speculation.

For George, the public vindication was a hollow victory. As he walked through town, he felt the loss of his family's support keenly. The Carter name, once a source of pride and privilege, now felt like a burden, a reminder of all he had sacrificed.

"I don't regret it," he told Hetty as they sat in her garden, a rare moment of peace in the chaos that had become their lives. "But I'd be lying if I said it didn't hurt. They're still my family, despite everything."

Hetty squeezed his hand, wishing she could ease his pain. "Your true family is here," she said softly. "Those who stand by you, who believe in what's right. We're your family now, George."

Their moment of tenderness was interrupted by Robert, who arrived breathless and wide-eyed. "You need to move," he said urgently. "Now. They're coming for the evidence."

In a flurry of activity, they gathered every document, every scrap of proof they had accumulated. As they worked, Robert explained in hurried whispers how he had overheard plans to destroy everything, to discredit their claims by eliminating the evidence.

"I can't openly support you," Robert said, his expression pained. "But I can't stand by and watch this injustice either. Be careful, George. They're desperate, and desperate men are dangerous."

They had just finished hiding the last of the documents when the sound of approaching footsteps sent them scrambling for cover. From their hiding place, they watched as a group of men, led by a figure they recognised as Dr Whitaker, searched the house.

"It's not here," Dr Whitaker growled after a fruitless search. "That little bitch and her friends must have moved it. Find them!"

As the men stomped out, Hetty and George exchanged a relieved glance. They had saved the evidence, but at what cost?

The following morning brought news that sent shockwaves through the town. Judge Harrow, one of the highest-ranking members of the resurrectionist ring, had been identified and arrested. But joy quickly turned to dismay as word spread that he had somehow escaped custody, vanishing into the night.

"This is bad," Frederick said as they gathered in the parlour of his home. "Harrow knows everything. If he talks to the right people, and makes the right deals..."

"Then all of this could have been for nothing," Hetty finished, her heart sinking.

The room fell silent, the weight of their situation pressing down upon them. They had come so far, risked so much, but victory still seemed frustratingly out of reach.

"So, what do we do now?" George asked, voicing the question on all their minds.

Hetty stood, her eyes blazing with determination.

Chapter Forty-Three

The Blackstone courthouse stood as a bastion of justice, its imposing facade a stark contrast to the tumultuous emotions swirling within its walls. For weeks, the trials of the resurrectionists had captivated the town, drawing crowds that spilled out onto the streets, eager for any morsel of information about the proceedings.

Hetty Morgan stood at the witness stand, her heart pounding but her voice steady as she recounted the events that had led to this moment. The sea of faces before her blurred into a single, expectant entity as she spoke of midnight raids, clandestine meetings, and the gradual unravelling of a conspiracy that had threaded its way through the very fabric of the town.

"And your father's involvement?" the prosecutor asked, his voice cutting through the hushed murmurs of the courtroom.

Hetty took a deep breath, her eyes finding Thomas Morgan's in the gallery. "My father was coerced," she stated firmly. "Threatened with his own life and mine if he didn't comply. He kept their books, yes, but he did so under extreme duress, always searching for a way to expose their crimes without putting me in danger."

As Hetty stepped down from the witness stand, her legs trembled slightly, the weight of her testimony pressing down upon her. She caught George's eye in the gallery, his encouraging nod steadying her nerves. The air in the courtroom felt thick with tension, the scent of nervous sweat mingling with the faint aroma of tobacco that clung to the judges' robes.

A voice from the public gallery rang out, "God bless you, Miss Morgan! You've done us all a service!"

The judge's gavel cracked sharply. "Silence in the court! Any further outbursts will result in immediate removal."

Hetty took her seat, her heart racing. She couldn't help but marvel at how far they'd come, from hushed conversations in darkened rooms to this public reckoning. As George took the stand, she found herself holding her breath, acutely aware of the stakes at play.

George Carter took the stand, his eyes swept the courtroom, landing briefly on his family seated in stony silence near the back. The pain of estrangement was etched in the tightness of his jaw, the slight tremor in his hands as he was sworn in.

"Dr Carter," the prosecutor began, "please tell the court about your discovery of the resurrectionist ring's activities."

George's testimony was damning. He spoke of overheard conversations, of documents discovered in his family's study, of the gradual realisation that the very pillars of Blackstone society were complicit in unspeakable crimes.

"And your father's involvement?" The question hung in the air, heavy with implication.

George hesitated, his gaze flickering to William Carter's impassive face. "My father was aware of the Society's activities," he said finally, his voice thick with emotion. "The extent of his involvement, I cannot say with certainty. But he knew, and he did nothing to stop it."

As George stepped down from the witness stand, the courtroom erupted into a cacophony of voices. The judge's gavel cracked against the bench, but it did little to quell the surge of emotions from the gallery.

"That's right, Dr. Carter! Tell 'em all!" shouted a gruff voice from the back.

A woman near the front stood up, her face flushed with anger. "How dare you betray your own family! Shame on you!"

"Order! I will have order in this court!" the judge bellowed, his face reddening with exertion.

But the crowd was not to be silenced so easily. A middle-aged man in a worn tweed jacket called out, "It's about time someone had the courage to speak the truth!"

"Courage? Ha!" retorted another voice. "More like a traitor to his class, if you ask me!"

The judge's gavel slammed down again. "If you cannot control yourselves, I will clear this courtroom!"

For a minute, a tense silence fell, but it was quickly broken by a clear, feminine voice. "God bless you, Miss Morgan! You've done us all a service!" It was the same woman who had spoken the same words just a moment before.

Hetty's cheeks flushed at the unexpected support, but before she could react, another voice rang out.

"Service? She's brought nothing but chaos to our town!"

"Silence!" the judge roared. "The next person to speak out of turn will be held in contempt of court!"

A murmur rippled through the crowd, but the threat of punishment seemed to have the desired effect. The bailiff moved to stand menacingly near the most vocal members of the gallery.

As the prosecutor prepared to call the next witness, an elderly woman stood up slowly, her voice quavering but determined. "Your Honour, if I may... I lost my grandson to these monsters. These young people," she gestured to Hetty and George, "they're fighting for all of us who couldn't fight for ourselves."

The judge's expression softened slightly. "Ma'am, while I sympathise with your loss, I must insist on maintaining order in this courtroom. Please be seated."

As the woman sat down, a ripple of respectful nods passed through the gallery. Even those who had been vocal in their opposition seemed subdued by her words.

The judge cleared his throat, his stern gaze sweeping across the courtroom. "Given the hour and the gravity of today's testimonies, this court will adjourn until tomorrow morning. I expect all parties to be present and prepared to continue at nine o'clock sharp."

As the gavel fell, signalling the end of the day's proceedings, a buzz of conversation erupted throughout the courtroom. The town of Blackstone, it seemed, was as divided as it was united by the revelations of the trial. Hetty and George exchanged a glance, both acutely aware that their actions had set in motion changes that would resonate far beyond the walls of this courtroom.

As George stepped down from the witness stand, the weight of his words seemed to press upon the entire room. He had chosen truth over family loyalty, justice over personal comfort. The cost of that choice was written into every line of his face.

Outside the courthouse, Frederick and Beatrice huddled together, their voices low and urgent.

"We can't leave anything to chance," Beatrice muttered, her eyes red-rimmed from lack of sleep. "These men have friends in high places. One mistake, one overlooked detail, and they could walk free."

Frederick nodded, squeezing her hand gently. "We won't let that happen. We've come too far to fail now. Let's go over the evidence for tomorrow's testimonies one more time."

In homes and taverns, citizens grappled with the day's revelations. Whispered conversations spoke of grave robberies, of the poor and vulnerable targeted for their bodies, of experiments that pushed far beyond the boundaries of ethical science. The full horror of the resurrectionist trade was only beginning to be laid bare, and tomorrow promised even more shocking disclosures.

Chapter Forty-Four

The courthouse buzzed with anticipation as the following day's proceedings began. The air was thick with tension, the wooden benches creaking under the weight of spectators eager for the next revelation in the resurrectionist trials. Today's focus: the untimely death of Archibald Pritchard.

Beatrice Pritchard sat rigidly in the front row, her fingers intertwined with Frederick's, both drawing strength from the other's presence. As Mr Grayson took the stand, a hush fell over the courtroom.

"Mr Grayson," the prosecutor began, his voice cutting through the silence, "you were the coroner who examined Mr Archibald Pritchard's body, were you not?"

Grayson nodded, his usual air of superiority somewhat diminished under the weight of scrutiny. "I was, yes."

"And you ruled his death an accident?"

"Based on the evidence available at the time, yes."

A murmur rippled through the crowd. From the back, a voice called out, "Liar! You knew what you were doing!"

The judge's gavel cracked like thunder. "Order! I will have order in this court, or I'll have it cleared!"

As the questioning continued, it became clear that Grayson's examination had been cursory at best, willfully negligent at worst. The prosecutor produced a series of documents, each more damning than the last.

"Mr Grayson, can you explain why you failed to note the injection mark on Mr Pritchard's neck? A mark consistent with the administration of a powerful sedative?"

Grayson's face paled. "I... I must have overlooked it."

"Overlooked it?" the prosecutor pressed. "Or deliberately ignored it?"

"Objection!" Grayson's lawyer interjected. "Speculation!"

"Sustained," the judge ruled. "Rephrase your question, Sir."

As the questioning continued, Frederick leaned in close to Beatrice. "Look at him squirm," he whispered. "Father would have enjoyed seeing this."

Beatrice squeezed his hand, a mix of grief and satisfaction etched on her face. "Your father always said the truth would come out. I only wish he were here to see it."

The prosecutor now held up a ledger. "Your Honour, I'd like to submit this as evidence. It's a record of payments made to Mr Grayson by the Society, coinciding with several suspicious deaths he ruled as accidents or natural causes."

The courtroom erupted. "Hang him!" someone shouted. "Justice for Archibald!"

The judge's gavel slammed down repeatedly. "Silence! The next person to speak out of turn will be removed from this courtroom!"

As order was restored, Grayson's composure crumbled. "I... I had no choice," he stammered. "They threatened my family. I didn't want to be part of it, but once you're in, there's no getting out."

"No choice?" Beatrice stood suddenly, her voice ringing out clear and strong. "My husband had no choice when your associates murdered him! He had no choice when you covered up their crime!"

"Mrs Pritchard, please be seated," the judge warned, though his tone was not unkind.

Frederick gently pulled his mother back down, but his eyes burned with a mixture of pride and long-suppressed anger.

The prosecutor turned back to Grayson. "Mr Grayson, did you or did you not knowingly falsify the report on Archibald Pritchard's death to protect the resurrectionist society?"

A heavy silence fell over the courtroom. Grayson's shoulders sagged, the fight going out of him. "I did," he whispered. "God forgive me, I did."

The admission sent shockwaves through the courtroom. Beatrice let out a choked sob, years of pent-up grief and anger finally finding release. Frederick wrapped an arm around her, his own eyes glistening with unshed tears.

As Grayson was led away, the judge called for a recess. In the chaos that followed, Hetty made her way to Beatrice and Frederick.

"Beatrice, Frederick," she said softly, "I know this won't bring Mr Pritchard back, but I hope it brings you some peace."

Beatrice clasped Hetty's hand. "Thank you, my dear. Your father will be proud of you, you know. As would Archibald."

As they left the courtroom, the weight of the day's revelations hung heavy in the air. Justice had been served, but the cost had been high. The resurrectionist trials were far from over, and more secrets were yet to be unveiled. But for now, Archibald Pritchard could rest easy, his name cleared and his murderers exposed.

Frederick looked up at the sky as they stepped outside. "We did it, Father," he murmured. "We did it."

Chapter Forty-Five

Dr Simmons, once Blackstone's most respected surgeons, broke down on the stand as he described the procedures they had performed. "We thought we were pushing the boundaries of medical science," he sobbed. "But we lost our humanity in the process."

The legitimate members of the Medical Society scrambled to distance themselves from the scandal. Statements were issued, denouncing the actions of their colleagues and pledging full cooperation with the authorities. But for many in Blackstone, the damage was done. The trust between doctor and patient, once sacred, had been irrevocably shattered.

Grace Pembroke's testimony came as a surprise to many. Gone was the haughty socialite, replaced by a young woman worn down by guilt and fear. She spoke of overheard conversations, of suspicions ignored, of a gradual entanglement in a web of lies and deceit.

"I was wrong," she said, her eyes seeking out Hetty and George in the courtroom. "I let jealousy and pride blind me to the truth. I spread rumours, tried to discredit you both. I can only ask for your forgiveness, though I know I don't deserve it."

Hetty felt a complex surge of emotions – pity, anger, a faint echo of empathy. George's hand found hers, a silent gesture of support and understanding.

As the trial progressed, the tension between George and his family became increasingly palpable. During a recess, Hetty found George standing alone in a quiet corridor, his shoulders slumped with the weight of his testimony.

"George," she said softly, approaching him with caution.

He turned, his eyes lighting up at the sight of her. "Hetty," he breathed, reaching for her hand.

"Are you alright?" she asked, searching his face.

George's laugh was hollow. "Alright? I've just testified against my own family, exposed years of corruption and crime. I'm not sure I'll ever be *'alright'* again."

Hetty squeezed his hand. "You did the right thing, George. It took immense courage."

"Did I?" he asked, his voice barely above a whisper. "Then why does it feel like I've destroyed everything?"

"Not destroyed," Hetty corrected gently. "Transformed. We're building something new, George. Something honest and just."

He nodded slowly, drawing strength from her words. As they stood there, hands entwined, the sounds of the courthouse faded away. For a

THE DAUGHTER'S ENDURING LOVE

moment, it was just the two of them, united in their pursuit of truth, no matter the cost.

Robert Carter's testimony provided the final nails in the coffin for the Pembrokes and their associates. He spoke of overheard conversations, of documents he had discovered while searching for the truth about his family's involvement. His words carried the weight of someone torn between family loyalty and moral obligation.

"I couldn't stand by and watch this injustice continue," he said, his voice steady despite the tension evident in his posture. "Regardless of personal cost, the truth had to come to light."

As the trials neared their conclusion, Hetty and George found their relationship tested by the relentless stress and public scrutiny. Moments of privacy were rare, each interaction scrutinised by a town hungry for any new development in the scandal that had rocked their community.

"Sometimes I do wonder if we did the right thing, whether what I said to you in the courthouse was true. Hetty confessed one evening, as they walked along the river's edge, away from prying eyes. "Look at the chaos we've caused, the lives upended."

George stopped, turning to face her. "Hetty, we didn't cause this chaos. We exposed it. The damage was already being done, hidden in the shadows. We brought it into the light where it could be confronted and healed."

She nodded, leaning into his embrace. "I know. It's just overwhelming sometimes. The weight of it all."

"We carry it together," George murmured into her hair.

"We're not the same people we were when this all started," Hetty mused, looking around at her friends. "For better or worse, this experience has shaped us."

George nodded, his arm around Hetty's shoulders. "We've seen the darkness that can lurk behind respectable facades. But we've also seen the courage of ordinary people standing up for what's right."

Chapter Forty-Six

In the Carter household, a reckoning was taking place that would shape the family's future. William Carter sat in his study, the weight of recent events pressing down upon him like a physical force. The leather of his chair creaked as he shifted, unable to find comfort in the familiar surroundings that had once been his sanctuary.

The estrangement from George, the public shame, the realisation of how far he had strayed from his own moral compass – it was almost too much to bear. His eyes, red-rimmed and weary, fell upon the family portrait on his desk. Happier times, when the world seemed simpler and his path clearer.

Margaret Carter approached her husband cautiously, her footsteps soft on the Persian rug. "William," she said softly, placing a gentle hand on his shoulder, "perhaps it's time we considered... reconciliation. George was right, after all. Maybe it's time we acknowledged that."

William looked up, his face a mask of conflict. "How can he ever forgive us, Margaret? How can we even begin to make amends?"

"We start by trying," Margaret replied, her voice firm but kind. "We start by admitting our mistakes and working to be better. It's not too late, William. Not if we don't want it to be."

William stood abruptly, pacing the room. "But he exposed us, this family. We will never be the same again. I'm not sure I want him anywhere near us."

"William Carter!" Margaret's voice sharpened. "Listen to yourself. This is our son we're talking about."

He turned to face her, his eyes brimming with unshed tears. "Don't you think I know that? Every day, I'm reminded of what we've lost, what I've thrown away with my pride and my... my foolishness."

Margaret softened, moving to stand before him. "My dear, dear William. Do you remember when we married? We promised each other we would do anything to protect our children, love them for who they are, stick together as a family no matter what damage may have been done."

William's shoulders sagged. "I remember," he whispered.

"So why is now any different? Yes, George may have gone about this the wrong way entirely. Maybe he should have consulted us sooner, given us a chance to rectify our wrongdoings. But George is George. And he has done what he believes is right for the citizens of the town. You cannot argue with that or reject him from this family out of principle."

William turned away, staring out the window at the manicured gardens below. "It's not just about principle, Margaret. It's about legacy, about the Carter name. How can we continue our lineage when our own son has..." he trailed off, unable to finish the thought.

Margaret moved to stand beside him, her reflection joining his in the glass. "Our legacy, William, is not just in our name or our social standing. It's in the values we instill in our children, the courage we show in facing our mistakes. George has shown remarkable courage. Perhaps it's time we showed some of our own."

William's jaw clenched. "And what of this... this wedding? To the undertaker's daughter, of all people. How can we possibly accept that?"

"Miss Morgan has shown herself to be a woman of great strength and character," Margaret replied. "Perhaps, instead of seeing her as a blemish on our family tree, we should see her as new growth, bringing fresh life and perspective."

For a long moment, William was silent, the ticking of the mantel clock marking the passage of time. Finally, he turned to his wife. "I don't know if I can do this, Margaret. I don't know if I have the strength."

Margaret cupped his face in her hands, her eyes filled with love and determination. "You do, my dear. You have more strength than you know. And you don't have to do it alone. We're in this together, remember?"

William nodded slowly, covering her hands with his own. "Together," he echoed.

Margaret smiled softly. "I'll leave you to your thoughts now. But William, remember – every moment we wait is another moment lost. Don't let pride rob you of the chance to know your son again."

As Margaret left the study, closing the door quietly behind her, William returned to his desk. He sat heavily in his chair, his gaze falling on the blank paper before him. With a trembling hand, he reached for his pen.

The scratching of nib against paper filled the room as William Carter began to write, pouring out his heart in ink. What the letter contained, only he knew, but as the words flowed, a sense of purpose seemed to settle over him. The future of the Carter family hung in the balance, and with each line, William was shaping what that future might be.

Chapter Forty-Seven

The morning sun bathed Blackstone in a warm, golden glow, as if nature itself was celebrating the union of Hetty Morgan and George Carter. The town buzzed with excitement, the air filled with the sweet scent of spring blossoms and the promise of new beginnings.

In Hetty's childhood home, a flurry of activity had taken over. Dressmakers fussed over last-minute alterations, while flower arrangements were carefully placed throughout the house. Amid the cheerful chaos, Hetty found a moment of quiet reflection in her father's study.

Thomas Morgan entered, his face etched with a mixture of joy and wistfulness. "Hetty, my dear," he said softly, "you look radiant."

Hetty turned, her eyes misting with emotion. "Oh, Father," she whispered, embracing him tightly.

As they pulled apart, Thomas held his daughter at arm's length, his gaze full of pride and love. "I never thought I'd see this day," he admitted. "After everything we've been through, to have a moment of such pure happiness is more than I could have hoped for."

Hetty squeezed her father's hands. "We've come through the darkness together, Father. And now, we step into the light."

Thomas nodded, a tear escaping down his cheek. "Your mother would have been so proud of you, Hetty. Not just for this day, but for everything you've done. Your courage, your unwavering pursuit of justice. You've become a woman of remarkable strength and compassion."

"I learned from the best," Hetty replied, her voice thick with emotion. "Father, I want you to know that even though I'm starting a new chapter with George, you'll always be a crucial part of my life. We're in this together, remember?"

Thomas pulled his daughter close once more. "Always, my dear. Always."

Meanwhile, at the Carter estate, George stood before the mirror, adjusting his cravat with trembling hands. A knock at the door startled him from his reverie.

"Come in," he called, expecting his brother Robert. To his surprise, it was his father, William Carter, who entered, his face a mask of conflicting emotions.

"Father," George breathed, his heart pounding. "I... I didn't expect to see you here today. I received your letter, I appreciate it. I know I could have exposed the truths in a more compassionate way, I know I should have spoken to you sooner, but we were running out of time."

"You don't need to explain yourself anymore. A father should be present on his son's wedding day," he said, his voice gruff with suppressed emotion. "No matter the... circumstances."

George swallowed hard, watching as his father reached out to straighten his already-perfect cravat. The gesture, so familiar yet now laden with unspoken tension, brought a lump to his throat.

"I know we don't see eye to eye, George," William continued, his hands falling to his sides. "But I will not have it said that a Carter abandoned his family, even in disagreement."

"Thank you, Father," George managed, the words barely audible.

William nodded curtly, then reached into his pocket, producing an envelope. "I had intended for Robert to give you this, but... well, here."

With shaking hands, George opened the letter. His father's bold handwriting filled the page:

'George,

On this, your wedding day, I find myself at a crossroads. Our disagreements run deep, and I cannot pretend they do not exist. Yet, you are my son, and that bond cannot be severed by mere difference of opinion.

Your choices have been your own, guided by a moral compass that, while foreign to me, I cannot help but respect. You have shown a courage and conviction that, though it pains me to admit, speaks to the man you have become.

I may not fully understand or approve of the path you have chosen, but know this: you carry the Carter name, and with it, my grudging respect for your fortitude.

May your union bring you the happiness you seek, and may you never have cause to regret the stands you have taken.

Your father,
William Carter'

George looked up, tears pricking at his eyes. "You'll be there?" he asked, hardly daring to hope.

William's jaw tightened, but he nodded. "I will. For the family. For appearances." A beat passed before he added, softer, "And for you, son."

As father and son stood in weighted silence, Margaret Carter appeared at the door, her eyes widening at the scene before her. "William," she breathed, "you came."

"Of course," William replied stiffly. "We are Carters. We stand together, even in... disagreement."

Margaret moved to George's side, squeezing his arm gently. "It's time," she said softly. "Are you ready?"

George nodded, straightening his shoulders. As they moved to leave, William's voice stopped them.

"George," he said, his tone inscrutable. "Whatever our differences... you'll make a fine husband."

The words hung in the air, a tentative olive branch extended across the chasm between them.

As the hour of the ceremony approached, Blackstone took on a festive air. Streets were decorated with bunting and flowers, and townsfolk in their Sunday best made their way to the church. The story of Hetty and George's fight against corruption had captured the town's imagination, transforming them into local heroes. Their wedding was seen as a symbol of Blackstone's renewal, a triumph of love and justice over darkness and deceit.

At the church, Frederick paced nervously, fiddling with the bouquet in his hands. When Beatrice appeared, resplendent in a gown of soft blue, his breath caught in his throat.

"Ma," he stammered, "you look absolutely stunning."

Beatrice blushed, a smile playing at her lips. "You clean up rather well yourself, son."

Inside the church, George stood at the altar, his heart racing as the wedding march began. As Hetty appeared at the entrance, a vision in white, a hush fell over the congregation. She seemed to float down the aisle on the arm of her father, her eyes locked with George's, both barely aware of the admiring murmurs that rippled through the crowd.

As Hetty reached the altar, George took her hands in his, marvelling at how perfectly they fit together. The minister began the ceremony, but for Hetty and George, the world had narrowed to just the two of them.

When it came time for their vows, George spoke first, his voice ringing clear and true through the church.

"Hetty, my love, my partner, my inspiration. You have been my strength in our darkest hours, my joy in our moments of triumph. I vow to stand by you, in all our adventures and challenges to come. To fight alongside you for justice, to cherish you in times of peace, to love you with every fibre of my being. Where you go, I go. Your battles are my battles. Your dreams are my dreams. From this day forward, we face the world together, as one."

Hetty's eyes shimmered with tears as she began her own vows.

"George, my dearest friend, my steadfast ally, my heart's true home. You have shown me the power of unwavering integrity, of standing firm in the face of adversity. I vow to be your support, your confidante, your greatest champion. To stand with you against injustice, to celebrate with you in moments of joy, to love you through all the chapters of our lives. Your cause is my cause. Your happiness is my happiness. Today, tomorrow, and always, we are united in love and purpose."

As the ceremony progressed, George couldn't help but glance towards the pews where his family sat. His mother's eyes shone with tears of joy, while Robert offered an encouraging smile. And there, stiff-backed and solemn, sat William Carter. Their eyes met for a brief moment, and George saw something flicker in his father's gaze – pride, perhaps, or a grudging respect.

The weight of that look stayed with George as he turned back to Hetty, his heart swelling with love and gratitude. Whatever challenges lay ahead, they would face them together, with the strength of their bond and the tentative hope of healing family rifts.

As they exchanged rings, sealing their vows, there wasn't a dry eye in the church. The minister's proclamation of their marriage was met with thunderous applause, the entire town seeming to rejoice in their union.

The reception that followed was a joyous affair. As Hetty and George moved among their guests, accepting congratulations and well-wishes, they overheard snippets of conversation that piqued their interest.

"...heard rumours of strange goings-on in London..."

"...whispers of a secret society, far-reaching and powerful..."

They exchanged glances, silently agreeing to revisit these hints later. Today was for celebration, but it seemed their work was far from over.

As the evening wore on, it came time for Hetty to throw her bouquet. With a laugh, she turned her back to the assembled unmarried women and tossed the flowers over her shoulder. To everyone's surprise and amusement, it was Frederick who caught the bouquet.

Finally, as the stars began to twinkle in the velvet sky, it was time for the newlyweds to depart. A magnificent carriage, bedecked with flowers and ribbons, waited to carry them off on their honeymoon journey.

As they climbed into the carriage, amid a shower of rice and cheers from the townspeople, Hetty and George found a moment of quiet togetherness.

"Well, Mrs Carter," George said, a smile playing at his lips, "are you ready for our next great adventure?"

Hetty's eyes sparkled with excitement. "More than ready, Dr Carter. Though I have a feeling our honeymoon might involve more mystery-solving than is traditional."

George laughed, pulling her close. "I wouldn't have it any other way. Those rumours we overheard... it seems our work is far from over."

As the carriage pulled away, the people of Blackstone waved and cheered. Hetty and George waved back, their hearts full of love for each other and for the town that had been their battleground and was now the foundation of their new life together.

But even as they set off towards new horizons, subtle undercurrents of tension rippled through the Carter family. Margaret watched the carriage disappear into the night, her joy for her son tinged with worry about the secrets still lurking in the shadows of their family history. And William stood next to his wife, his arm firmly around her waist with the weight of unspoken truths pressing down upon him.

Epilogue

Twelve months had passed since Hetty and George had bid farewell to the smoky streets of Blackstone. The gentle breeze rustling through the trees of Holly Village carried with it the sweet scent of wildflowers, a far cry from the acrid air they'd left behind.

Hetty sat on a checkered blanket spread across their modest garden, watching as George cradled their three month old daughter, Elizabeth. The baby's laughter, bright and pure, floated on the air as George tickled her chubby cheeks.

"She has your eyes," George said, looking up at Hetty with a smile that still made her heart skip a beat.

THE DAUGHTER'S ENDURING LOVE 227

"And your curiosity," Hetty replied, reaching out to stroke Elizabeth's downy head. "She's always watching, always learning."

As if on cue, Thomas Morgan emerged from the cottage, his arms laden with wooden blocks. "Speaking of learning," he said, setting the blocks down on the blanket, "I've finished these for your class, Hetty."

Hetty beamed at her father. The past year had brought changes for all of them, but perhaps none so dramatic as Thomas' transformation. Gone was the haunted look that had shadowed his eyes in Blackstone. Here in Holly Village, he'd found a new purpose, his skillful hands now crafting furniture and toys instead of coffins.

"Thank you, Father," Hetty said, examining the brightly painted letters and numbers on the blocks. "The children will love these."

Her small class of village children had started as a way to fulfill her long-held dream of teaching, but it had grown into something more. It was a way to give back to the community that had welcomed them so warmly, to help shape young minds free from the shadows of their past.

George set Elizabeth down on the blanket, where she immediately reached for one of the colorful blocks. "Your mother would be proud," he said softly to Hetty. "Of all of us."

Hetty nodded, blinking back tears. "I think she would. We've come so far."

As the sun began to set, painting the sky in hues of pink and gold, the small family made their way back into the cottage. The cozy home, filled with the scent of baking bread and the warmth of love, was a far cry from the undertaker's workshop where Hetty had grown up.

Later that evening, as George and Hetty sat by the fireplace, Elizabeth sleeping peacefully in her cradle nearby, Hetty reflected on their journey.

"Do you ever miss it?" she asked. "The excitement, the mystery?"

George took her hand, his thumb tracing gentle circles on her palm. "Sometimes," he admitted. "But then I look at you, at Elizabeth, at the life we've built here, and I know we made the right choice. And your father is so incredibly happy. It was one of the best decisions we made, asking him to come and live with us."

Hetty leaned into him, feeling the steady beat of his heart. "It was," she agreed. "Though I can't help but wonder about those rumours from London..."

George pressed a kiss to her forehead. "Whatever comes, we'll face it together. But for now, let's just enjoy this peace we've found."

As they sat there, wrapped in each other's arms, Hetty felt a profound sense of contentment wash over her. They had weathered storms, uncovered truths, and fought for justice. Now, in this quiet village, they had found something just as valuable – a chance to build a future filled with love, hope, and the promise of new beginnings.

About the author

I hope you enjoyed The Daughter's Enduring Love.

If you haven't yet read the rest of The Victorian Love Sagas, you can find the series here: https://mybook.to/VictorianLoveSagas

My FREE book, ***The Whitechapel Angel***, is also available for download here: https://dl.bookfunnel.com/xs5p4d0oog

About the Author:

I have always been passionate about historical romance set in the Victorian era. I love to place myself on the dark, murky streets of London and wonder what it would have been like to overcome tragedy and poverty to find true love. The different classes of society intrigue me and I'm fascinated to know if love ever truly prevailed between the working and upper class.

I'm not sure about you, but whenever I visit the streets of Whitechapel, or read historical books from the bygone era, I find myself transported back to a time when I once lived there myself. Some say past lives are a myth, past life transgression is a 'load of tosh,' and you only ever live this life in the now. But whether you believe in past lives or not, for me, I easily feel myself living in those times.

With each book, I strive to create stories that capture the heart and imagination of my readers, bringing to life the strong, resilient characters that live in that bygone era.

When not writing, I can be found exploring the great outdoors with my husband Mike, and my Jack Russell, Daisy, or curled up with a good book. There is nothing quite like lighting the log burner and a candle or two, and turning the pages.

Stay connected:

Please, if you have any feedback, email me at anneliesemmckay@gmail.com (my admin assistant,) and I will respond to all of you personally.

Printed in Great Britain
by Amazon